"Mistress," Nikolai slotted in, cool as ice.

"But we don't even know each other," Ella framed dazedly. "You're a stranger."

"If you live with me I won't be a stranger for long," Nikolai pointed out with monumental calm.

The very sound of that inhuman calm forced her to flip round and settle distraught eyes on his lean, darkly handsome face. "You can't be serious about this."

"I assure you that I am deadly serious. Move in and I'll forget your family's debts."

"But it's a *crazy* idea!" she gasped, floundering against his restrained silence. It was obvious that he was determined to behave as though such a proposition was an everyday occurrence.

"It's not crazy to me," Nikolai asserted. "When I want anything, I go after it hard and fast."

Did he want her like that? Enough to trace her, buy up her father's debts and try to buy rights to her body along with those debts? The very idea of that made her dizzy and plunged her brain into even greater turmoil. "It's immoral...it's blackmail—"

"It's definitely *not* blackmail. I'm giving you the benefit of a choice you didn't have before I came through that door," Nikolai Drakos fielded with glittering cool. "That choice is yours to make."

Dear Reader,

I can't quite believe this is my 100th book for Harlequin Presents! It's been an incredible experience, made all the more special by the wonderful editors, writers and readers I've met along the way.

As you may have guessed, this book is a very special one for me. When my editor gave me carte blanche on the story, I couldn't resist coming back to my favorite themes. There's something about a mistress story—especially when the hero is as commanding and determined as Nikolai Drakos is!

It's the moment when the hero realizes that he's got more than he bargained for with the heroine... or maybe it's when he realizes just how much he has to make amends for that I can never wait to get to write. Perhaps it's because finally the heroine is going to get the true love that she absolutely deserves. Either way, I couldn't think of anything that I wanted to write more than *Bought for the Greek's Revenge* for my 100th book.

It was a joy to write from start to finish, and I hope that you love it as much as I do.

Much love,

Lynne

xx

Lynne Graham

BOUGHT FOR THE GREEK'S REVENGE

"Lynne Graham's Harlequin Presents books have irresistible alpha males, incredible heroines and romance to make your heart race, and her 100th book, *Bought for the Greek's Revenge*, is no different. Seductive, sexy, passionate—a must-read!"

—SUSAN MALLERY

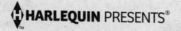

HARLEQUIN PRESENTS®

Recycling programs
for this product may
not exist in your area.

ISBN-13: 978-0-373-13439-7

Bought for the Greek's Revenge

First North American Publication 2016

Copyright © 2016 by Lynne Graham

This is a work of fiction. Names, characters, places and incidents are either the product of the author's imagination or are used fictitiously, and any resemblance to actual persons, living or dead, business establishments, events or locales is entirely coincidental.

This edition published by arrangement with Harlequin Books S.A.

For questions and comments about the quality of this book, please contact us at CustomerService@Harlequin.com.

Printed in U.S.A.

www.Harlequin.com

Lynne Graham was born in Northern Ireland and has been a keen romance reader since her teens. She is very happily married to an understanding husband who has learned to cook since she started to write! Her five children keep her on her toes. She has a very large dog who knocks everything over, a very small terrier who barks a lot, and two cats. When time allows, Lynne is a keen gardener.

Books by Lynne Graham

Harlequin Presents

The Sicilian's Stolen Son
Leonetti's Housekeeper Bride
The Secret His Mistress Carried
The Dimitrakos Proposition
A Ring to Secure His Heir
Unlocking Her Innocence

The Notorious Greeks

The Greek Demands His Heir
The Greek Commands His Mistress

Bound by Gold

The Sheikh's Secret Babies
The Billionaire's Bridal Bargain

The Legacies of Powerful Men

Ravelli's Defiant Bride
Christakis's Rebellious Wife
Zarif's Convenient Queen

A Bride for a Billionaire

A Rich Man's Whim
The Sheikh's Prize
The Billionaire's Trophy
Challenging Dante

Visit the Author Profile page at Harlequin.com for more titles.

For my readers who have given me endless support throughout my career, thank you.

CHAPTER ONE

Nikolai Drakos scanned the photo with a frown and enhanced it. It couldn't be the same woman; it simply couldn't be! There was no way that his quarry, Cyrus Makris, could possibly be planning to marry a woman from a humble background.

Bemused, Nikolai lifted his arrogant dark head high and once again studied the picture of the ethereal red-head. No way could it be the same little temptress he had once met working as a parking attendant. The world wasn't that small. Even so, he was aware that Cyrus owned a country house in Norfolk. A deeper frown lodged between his level dark brows, his quick and clever brain taking a rare hike into the recent past.

For all her diminutive size the woman he had met had had attitude, lots and *lots* of attitude, certainly not an attribute Nikolai sought from the transient beauties who shared his bed. But she had also had aquamarine eyes and a mouth as soft, silky and pink as a lotus blossom. A sizzling physical combination, which had taken a hell of a lot of forgetting on his part. His wide sensual mouth compressed with dissatisfaction. After she had blown him off, another man might have tried to find her again to make another attempt but Nikolai had refused to do so. He didn't chase women, he didn't do sweet talk or dates or flowers or any of that stuff *ever*. He walked away. The mantra by which he lived insisted that no woman was irreplaceable, no woman unique, and he didn't believe in love. She had simply caught his imagination for a few intoxicating moments but he had refused to allow lust to seduce him into pursuit. Since when had he had to pursue a woman?

And although it was generally known that Cyrus's elderly father was putting pressure on his forty-five-year-old son and heir to take a bride, it was a challenge to credit that Cyrus *could* be planning to marry the feisty little redhead who had scratched the paint-work on Nikolai's cherished McLaren Spider. Besides, only pure and untouched female flesh excited Cyrus, as Nikolai's late sister had learned to her cost. And no way could that sparkling little redhead still be that pure and untouched.

Flexing his lean muscles as he sprang upright, Nikolai swept up the file he had been studying. The investigator he used was a consummate professional and the report would be thorough. He studied the photos afresh. He was willing to admit that the likeness between the two women was startling. Curiosity at a height, he began to read about Prunella, known as Ella. Yes, that night he had definitely heard her boss using that name, he conceded grimly. Ella Palmer, aged twenty-three, a former veterinary student who had once been engaged to Cyrus's dead nephew, Paul. Now there was a connection he could not have foreseen for Cyrus, who rarely bothered with relatives.

Nikolai read on, unexpectedly hungry for the details. It had been a year since the nephew had died of leukaemia and two years since Ella's father, George Palmer, had had a stroke. The older man was currently drowning in debt. Nikolai marvelled that Cyrus, who was rich but tight, had not stepped in to help Ella's family, but perhaps he was holding that possibility in reserve as a power play.

Nikolai, on the other hand, immediately grasped that it was *his* optimum moment for action and intervention. He called his team of personal assistants and issued his instructions even while he was still struggling to work out why Ella Palmer could be in line to become Cyrus's bride.

What was so special about her? For a couple of years at least she had evidently hovered on the outskirts of Cyrus's life. As his nephew's fiancée she would have been untouchable, the unattainable always a powerful temptation to a male who thrived on the challenge of breaking the rules. Now she was alone and unprotected and Cyrus appeared to be playing a waiting game. However, it was equally possible that Ella was eager to marry Cyrus, because although he was old enough to be her father he was also a prominent, and wealthy, businessman.

But what, other than innocence, could be attracting Cyrus? Ella Palmer had neither money nor connections to offer. She was a beauty, but could a formerly engaged young woman *still* be a virgin in this day and age? Nikolai shook his arrogant dark head in wonderment. Was that even possible? And had she the smallest concept of the kind of male she was dealing with? A man who was excited by sexual violence? And who, given the opportunity, would cause her irreparable harm? Would she consider a wedding ring adequate compensation for brutal mistreatment?

Whatever, Nikolai's objective was to take her off Cyrus. Cyrus was a dangerous man and Nikolai knew exactly how addicted he was to the seamier side of life. By utilising bribery, intimidation and hush money, Cyrus had so far contrived to escape justice. Nikolai had long been forced to pursue a more subtle form of revenge. Being both extremely rich and extremely clever, Nikolai had tracked his quarry's every move in the business world and had regularly snatched lucrative deals from right under Cyrus's nose. That had been easy because Cyrus was better at making enemies than keeping friends and making connections. But it wasn't nearly as satisfying as striking out at Cyrus on a more personal level would be. Losing Ella Palmer, seeing her choose his greatest rival over him, would really hit Cyrus hard where it hurt. And anything that caused Cyrus pain made Nikolai happy.

As for how his actions would affect Ella Palmer and her family, Nikolai ruminated darkly, did he really care? They would simply be collateral damage in Nikolai's battle. But, at the same time, her family would be freed from crippling debt while Ella would be protected from Cyrus. Nikolai's burning desire for revenge was fuelled by ruthless resolution and by the knowledge that all Cyrus's victims had been cruelly denied justice. Yet there was also a weird personal feel to the challenge that made his teeth grit because, try as he did to stay cool and in control and essentially uninvolved, unholy rage gripped Nikolai at the thought of Cyrus getting his slimy hands on Ella and *hurting* her…

* * *

'It's bad, Ella,' Gramma said heavily.

'How bad?' Ella prompted, dry-mouthed.

George Palmer, Ella's father and Gramma's son, sighed heavily. 'I'm a terrible failure of a man when it comes to my family… I've lost everything.'

'The business, yes…perhaps it's too late for anything to be saved there, but that doesn't make you a failure,' Ella conceded in a wobbly voice, because they had known for ages that the shop was doing badly. 'But, at least, the house—'

'*No*, Ella,' Gramma cut in, her lined face pale and stiff with self-discipline. 'This time the house has to go as well—'

'But how can that be?' Ella exclaimed incredulously. '*You* own the house, not Dad!'

'My divorce from Joy took half the business,' the older man reminded her.

'And the house was the only asset we had left. Your father couldn't get the business loan he needed to pay off Joy without backing it up with the house,' Ella's grandmother, Gramma, a petite white-haired lady in her seventies, told her tightly. 'So, we put the house on the line and hoped for the best.'

'Oh, my…goodness,' Ella gasped after carefully searching for a word that would not make her grandmother flinch.

Thinking of her stepmother, the volatile Joy, Ella tried to reflect on the reality that since the divorce her father was a much happier man. His wife had been a very demanding woman, and although the older man had made a decent recovery from the stroke that had laid him low two years earlier, he now used a stick and the left side of his body remained weak. His wife, Joy, had walked out on him during his rehabilitation. She had deserted him as soon as his once comfortable income had declined. Her father had not been able to afford the services of a good lawyer in the divorce that followed and it had been a shock when his estranged wife had been awarded half the value of his furniture shop in the settlement. That pay out had led them straight into their current dire financial straits.

'Taking that risk with the house hasn't worked out for us but I'm trying to console myself with the idea that at least we *tried*,' George Palmer said wryly. 'If we hadn't tried we would always have wondered if we should have done. Now it's done and dusted and, unhappily for us, my creditors need to be paid.'

Ella's mood was not improved by the older man's accepting attitude. George Palmer was one of nature's gentlemen and he never had a bad word to say about anyone or anything. Her attention fell instead on the letter lying on the kitchen table and she snatched it up. 'That's what this is about? Your creditors?'

'Yes, my debts have been sold on to another organisation. That's a letter from the new owner's solicitors telling me that they want to put the house on the market.'

'Well, we'll just see about that!' Ella snapped, scrambling upright and pulling out her phone, eager to be able to do something at last, for sitting around bemoaning bad situations was not her style.

'This is business, Ella.' Gramma gave her feisty grandchild a regretful appraisal. 'Appealing to business people is a waste of your time. All they want is their money and hopefully a profit out of their investment.'

'It's not that simple…it's our *lives* you're talking about!' Ella proclaimed emotively, stalking out of the kitchen to ring the legal firm and ask for an appointment.

Life could be so very cruel, she was thinking. Time and time again misfortune and disappointment had made Ella suffer and she had become so accustomed to that state of affairs that she had learned to swallow hard and bear it. But when it came to her family suffering adversity, well, that was something else entirely and it brought out her fighting spirit. Her father couldn't regain his full health but he did deserve some peace after the turmoil of his divorce. She couldn't bear him to lose his home when he had already been forced to adjust to so many frightening changes.

And what about Gramma? Tears flooded Ella's bright green eyes when she thought of Gramma losing her beloved home. Gramma's late husband had moved her into this house as a bride in the nineteen sixties. Her son had been born below this roof and she had never lived anywhere else. Neither had Ella or her father, Ella reflected wretchedly. The worn but comfortable detached house sat at the very heart of their sense of security.

George Palmer had fallen in love with Ella's mother, Lesley, at university and had hoped to marry her when she became pregnant with Ella. Lesley, however, had been less keen and shortly after Ella's birth she had left George and her daughter behind to pursue a career in California. A brilliant young physicist, Ella's mother had since gone on to become a world-renowned scientist.

'I obviously lack both the mum and the wife gene

because I have no regrets over being single and child-free even now,' Lesley had told Ella frankly when they first met when Ella was eighteen. 'George adored you and, when he married Joy, I assumed it would be better for me to leave you to be part of a perfect little family *without* my interference...'

Ella dragged her mind back from that ironic little speech that she had received from her uncaring mother. Lesley hadn't recognised that her complete lack of interest in Ella and absence of regret would hurt her daughter even more. In addition, George, Joy and Ella had not been a perfect family because as soon as Joy had become George's wife she had made her resentment of Ella's presence in their home very obvious. Had it not been for George's and Gramma's love and attention, Ella would have been a deeply unhappy child.

And Joy, Ella thought bitterly, had done very nicely out of the divorce, thank you. However, she cleared her mind of such futile reflections and concentrated on thinking instead about her family's predicament while she outlined her request to the very well-spoken young man who accepted her call after she had been passed through several people at the legal firm. She was dismayed to then walk into a solid brick wall of silence. With a polite reference to client confidentiality, the solicitor refused to tell her who her father's creditor was and pointed out that nobody would be prepared to discuss her father's debts with anyone other than her father, although he did at least promise to pass on her request.

As she replaced the phone and checked her watch in dismay Ella's eyes were stinging with tears of frustration, but she had to pull herself together and get to work, her small income being the only money currently entering the household aside of Gramma's pension. As she pulled on her jacket an idea struck her and she paused in the kitchen doorway to look at the two older people. 'You know…er…have you thought of approaching Cyrus for help?' she asked abruptly.

Her father's face stiffened defensively. 'Ella… I—'

'Cyrus is a family friend,' Gramma stepped in to acknowledge. 'It would be very wrong to approach a friend in such circumstances simply because he has money.'

A flush of colour drenched Ella's heart-shaped face and she nodded respectful agreement, even though she was tempted to remark that matters were serious enough to risk causing offence. Perhaps her relatives had already asked and been refused help or perhaps they knew something she didn't, she conceded uncomfortably. In any case approaching Cyrus was not currently possible because Cyrus was abroad on a lengthy trade-delegation tour of China.

She climbed into the ancient battered van that was her only means of transport. Butch went into a cacophony of barking on the doorstep and she blinked, very belatedly recalling her pet, who normally went to work with her. She braked and opened the car door in a hurry to scoop the little animal up.

Butch was a Chihuahua/Jack Russell mix and absolutely tiny, but he had the heart and personality of a much bigger dog. He had been born with only three legs and would have been euthanised at birth had Ella not fallen in love with him while she had been working on a placement at a veterinary surgery. He settled down quietly into his pet carrier, knowing that his owner frowned on any kind of disturbance while she was driving.

Ella worked at an animal sanctuary only a few miles from her home. She had volunteered at Animal Companions as a teenager, found solace there while the man she loved had slowly succumbed to the disease that would eventually kill him and had ended up working at the rescue centre when she had been forced to leave her veterinarian course before its completion. One day she still hoped to be able to finish her training and become a fully qualified veterinary surgeon with her own practice, but Paul's illness and her father's stroke had been inescapable events that had thrown her life plan off course.

Not such a bad thing, she often told herself bracingly at times when it seemed that her desire to work as an animal doctor was continually destined to collapse in the face of other people's needs. She had gained a lot of experience working at the rescue centre and was using the skills she had acquired during her training by functioning as an unofficial veterinary nurse. To think any other way when her presence at home had achieved so much good would be unforgivably selfish, she told herself firmly. Gramma and her dad had badly needed her assistance during that testing time. And she was painfully aware of all the advantages that their loving support had given *her*.

Her boss, Rosie, a generous-hearted woman in her forties with frizzy blonde curls, surged out to the car park to greet Ella. 'You'll never believe it… Samson's got a home!' she gasped excitedly.

Ella started to smile. 'You're kidding—'

'Well, I haven't done the home visit yet to check

them out but they did seem very genuine people. Just lost their own dog to old age, so I didn't think they'd want another oldie but they're afraid that a young dog could be too much for them to handle,' Rosie told her.

'Samson really deserves a good home,' Ella said fondly, for the thirteen-year-old terrier had been repeatedly passed over because of his age by other prospective owners.

'He's a very loving little chap...' Rosie paused, her warm smile dwindling. 'I heard your father's shop closed down last week. I'm so sorry for your dad—'

'Well, can't be helped,' Ella responded, hoping to forestall further comment because she couldn't discuss her family's financial affairs with Rosie, who was a hopeless gossip.

While Rosie talked about the rise of the big furniture chain stores working to the detriment of smaller businesses, Ella made polite sounds of agreement while she checked that the kennel staff had completed their early morning cleaning routine. That done, Ella put on overalls and concentrated on sorting out an emaciated stray with matted hair brought to them by the council dog warden. When she had finished she peeled off the overalls, washed and fed the poodle mix and settled her down in a run.

She heard a car and assumed that Rosie had set off to do her home visit to check out Samson's new potential owners. She went into the office where she worked between times, being better at paperwork than Rosie, who was more driven by her need to rescue animals and re-home them than by the equally important requirement of meeting all of a recognised charity's medical, legal and financial obligations. As a team, however, she and

Rosie were efficient because their abilities fitted neatly together. Rosie was fantastic at dealing with the public and fundraising while Ella preferred to work with the animals in the background.

Indeed Ella had been very uncomfortable at the fancy charity auction that Cyrus had persuaded her to attend with him only a month earlier. Champagne, high heels and evening dresses were really not her thing. But how could she have said no when Cyrus had been so very good to Paul while he was ill? Acting as Cyrus's partner at a couple of social occasions was little enough to be asked to do in return, she ruminated wryly, wondering as she often had why Cyrus had never married. He was forty-five years old, presentable, successful and single. Once or twice she had wondered if he was gay but Paul had got very annoyed at her for trying to make something out of what he insisted was nothing.

Rosie entered the office, rudely springing Ella from her momentary loss of concentration. The older woman looked flustered. 'You have a visitor,' she announced.

Her smooth brow furrowing, Ella stood up and moved round the desk. 'A visitor?' she prompted in surprise.

'He's a *foreigner*,' Rosie stage-whispered as if that fact were terribly mysterious and unusual.

'But he went to school in the UK and speaks excellent English,' a very masculine voice commented from the door that still stood open on the small outer hall, where he had evidently been left to hover.

Ella's lower limbs succumbed to nervous paralysis as she froze where she stood, a tiny disbelieving quiver running down her spine because, incredibly, she *recognised* that voice even though she had only heard it on one previous occasion almost a year earlier. It couldn't be but it was…it was *him*, the gorgeous guy with the fancy car and the very short temper and the eyes that reminded her of melted caramel. What on earth was he doing visiting her at Animal Companions? Had he tracked her down?

'I'll just leave you in…er…privacy,' Rosie pronounced awkwardly, backing out of the office again as the very tall, dark man behind her strode forward without taking any apparent note of her still-lingering presence.

Rosie arched a pale brow. 'Do we need privacy?' she asked doubtfully.

Nikolai studied her fixedly. She was incredibly tiny and delicate in build. He remembered that. He remembered the long curling tangle of her bronze-coloured hair as well because the shade was unusual, neither brown nor red but a metallic shade somewhere between the two. She bore a ridiculously close resemblance to a pixie he had once seen in a fairy-story book, he thought, feeling oddly numb, oddly dry-mouthed as his keen dark gaze roved over her, reluctant to miss out on a single detail of that petite, pixeish perfection. No, of course she wasn't perfect, no woman was, he reasoned, striving to be more lucid, but that flawless porcelain skin, those glorious green eyes and that lush mouth in that beautiful face were quite unforgettable. Memory hadn't exaggerated her beauty, but his brain had persuaded him he had to prevent himself from chasing after her, he decided in exasperation.

'We do,' Nikolai confirmed, firmly shutting the door in Rosie's wake. 'We weren't introduced at our last meeting.'

'No, you were far too busy shouting at me,' Ella reminded him doggedly.

'My name is Nikolai Drakos and you are?'

As he extended a hand Gramma's strict upbringing brought Ella's own hand out to grip his. 'Prunella Palmer. Most people call me Ella. What are you doing here, Mr Drakos? Or are you here about that stupid car?' she asked witheringly.

'You pranged that stupid car,' Nikolai pointed out, unamused.

'I inflicted a minuscule rubbing mark on one wing. I didn't dent or scratch it,' she traded drily. 'I can't believe you're still complaining about it. Nobody got hurt and no real damage was done.'

Nikolai was very tempted to tell her how much that 'rubbing' mark had cost to remove. She had scraped the car past a bush when she'd accelerated too fast. His teeth ground together. It was healthy to be reminded just how very annoying she could be, he told himself warningly. Complaining? He had never complained in his life, not when his father beat him up, not when he was bullied at school, not even when his sister and only living relative had died. He had learnt at a very young age that basically nobody cared what happened to him and nobody was interested enough to listen to what he had endured. Nothing in life had ever come easy to Nikolai.

Ella couldn't take her eyes off him. He was so physically large in both height and breadth that he ate up every inch of space in Rosie's little office and made it feel crowded and suffocating. Tension held her rigid while she watched him like a rabbit mesmerised by a hawk ready to swoop down on her. Nikolai Drakos—

the ultimate female fantasy with olive skin, black hair and spectacular dark eyes. His tailored charcoal-grey business suit couldn't hide the reality that he was built with an athlete's lean, muscular power and he moved with long-legged easy grace, she registered, struggling to pinpoint exactly what continually drew her attention to him. He was very, very good-looking but it wasn't just the looks. He had amazing bone structure though and would probably still be turning heads in his sixties. Maybe it was the electrifying quality of the raw, masculine sex appeal he exuded. Twelve months earlier his sheer charisma had struck her like a thunderbolt and utterly humiliated her.

'I'm not here about the car,' Nikolai said very drily. 'I'm here because you *asked* to see me...'

Ella was thoroughly disconcerted by that statement. 'I don't know what you're talking about. How could I ask to see you when I have no way of contacting you? And why would I contact you when I haven't had the slightest desire to see you again?' she enquired tartly, her whole bearing suggesting that such a belief could only have come from an intolerable egotist.

A sardonic smile curved Nikolai's wide sensual mouth as he gazed down at her with scantily leashed satisfaction. *She* had approached *him*. She had come looking for him first and that felt very much like the helpful hand of fate working on his behalf.

'You did request my attention,' he told her again.

Bewilderment gripped Ella but it was swiftly followed by a surge of frustrated fury. So far she had been having a very bad day and she was not in the mood for big arrogant male surprises and particularly not one who had offended her by offering her a one-night stand before he had even enquired what her name was! Yes, act first, *think* afterwards, that was how Nikolai Drakos functioned around women, she reflected scornfully. He had made her feel bad about herself and she allowed no man to do that to her. Yet when she gazed back at him and rated the uncompromising light in his eyes and the hard resolution etched in his strong-boned features, she could suddenly see that he was not the weak, frivolous and impulsive male she had first assumed him to be and that threw her off balance…badly.

'I've had enough of this nonsense!' she told him bluntly. 'I want you to leave.'

Nikolai compounded his sins by slowly raising a beautifully drawn ebony brow. 'I don't think so.'

The rage that Ella always struggled to control broke through her cracking composure because she hated bullies and it seemed to her that he was trying to intimidate her. 'I *know* so!' she slammed back at him, half an octave higher. 'And if you're not out of here by the time I count to ten, I'm calling the police!'

'Go right ahead,' Nikolai advised, lodging his wide-shouldered frame back against the door and folding his arms with the infuriatingly cool poise of a male who had no intention of going anywhere. As she almost bounced in fury, she reminded him of a hummingbird dive-bombing a flower. Tiny but also colourful, intense and vibrant.

An unholy flash of hostility lit up Ella's emerald-green eyes. 'I mean it!'

Nikolai sighed. 'You only *think* you mean it. Be aware that that temper of yours is a major weakness.'

Incensed by that crack, Ella said, *'One—'*

'When you allow yourself to lose your head, you surrender control.'

'*Two*—'

'And you're not thinking rationally either,' Nikolai told her smoothly.

'*Three!*'

'How could you be?' Nikolai continued. 'Right now I can read your face like a map. You want to jump on me and thump me but you're not physically up to that challenge, so you're stuck acting illogical and child-ish—'

'*Four!* And shut up while I'm counting! *Five!*' Ella added jerkily, her throat muscles so tight, she could barely get the words out.

'The performance you're putting on for me now is why I never allow myself to lose my temper,' Niko-lai told her, thoroughly enjoying himself for the first time in a long time because she was that easy to rile. He would be able to wind her up like a clockwork toy and control her...*so* easily.

'Of course, you could try asking yourself why you're being this unreasonable. As far as I'm aware I did nothing worthy of this reception,' Nikolai murmured smooth as glass, his wide, expressive mouth quirking round the edges.

'*Six!*' But that fast she remembered his mouth on hers, hard and demanding and passionate, rather than playful and shy and sweet. He was the only man apart from Paul to ever kiss her. The core of steel deep in-side her reached a furnace heat of hatred and temper and shame but her body still betrayed her. Her nipples pinched into tight little buttons that stung, and lower down in a place she didn't even want to think about she felt that almost forgotten liquid, hot, sliding sensation. It made her teeth grind together in vexation.

'Seven!' she launched and reached for the phone on the desk, almost desperate to see him go, her brain a morass of angry, tumbling impressions and images.

'We're going to get on like a house on fire…*literally,*' Nikolai told her with sardonic bite. 'Because while I may control my temper, I am demanding, stubborn and impatient and if you cross me you'll know about it.'

'Out!' she spat at him furiously, outraged by the fact that she couldn't get him to react to her threat in even the smallest way. 'Get out of here!'

'Eight…maybe even nine,' Nikolai pronounced for her. 'When you know why I'm here, you'll *beg* me to stay.'

'In your dreams…*ten*!' Ella countered in a ringing tone of finality as she lifted the phone with a flourish.

'I'm the man who bought your father's debts,' Nikolai admitted and watched her freeze and lose all her animated angry colour while her arm slowly lowered the phone back on its rest and her hand fell back from it in dismay.

CHAPTER TWO

'THAT'S NOT POSSIBLE,' Ella whispered unevenly. 'It would be too much of a coincidence.'

'Coincidences happen,' Nikolai countered, for he had no intention of taking her into his confidence and sharing his ultimate plan.

'Not one this unlikely,' Ella argued, backing away from the desk while her brain endeavoured to regroup to this most surprising change of circumstance.

'You rang the firm who handle my legal work and asked to see me,' he reminded her levelly. 'Here I am.'

'I wasn't prepared for a personal visit, maybe a phone call or an appointment,' she muttered uncertainly, barely knowing what she was saying because the temper that was often her strength had subsided in fear like a pricked balloon. No, she couldn't possibly shout at or drive off her father's main creditor. Even angry, she wasn't that stupid.

The silence lay between them as thick and heavy as treacle. She stared at him, incredulous at such a piece of unwelcome happenstance as the combination of events that had brought Nikolai Drakos back into her life again. A man she had naturally assumed she would never see again, a man she had *prayed* she would never see again! And she had preferred that reality, had needed to know she could bury that silly little episode and wipe it from her mind as an insane moment while she was still grieving for the man she had loved. Being confronted by him again was a real slap in the face and she could feel her face warming and prickling as though she had sunburn.

'As you say...here you are,' Ella acknowledged woodenly. 'You can't be surprised that I'm shocked that my father's creditor is someone I've met before.'

'Would you call it a meeting? A brief encounter in a car park would be more accurate,' Nikolai murmured with a dry mockery that made her yearn to knock his teeth down his throat, for he made it sound as though they had shared rather more than a kiss.

And had she been willing, they would have done. She had no doubt of that. He was a player, the kind of male who did what he wanted when he wanted and he had certainly been in the mood for sex. Her face flamed at the awareness that, had she agreed and had it been physically possible, they could well have enjoyed a sordid, sweaty encounter there and then in his car and she would never have made it back to the misleading respectability of the hotel he had suggested. Inwardly she cursed her fair skin as mortification burned her cheeks, while he studied her with a measured attention that warned her he was picking up on her every reaction.

'So, you own Dad's debts,' Ella recapped, striving to push onward past the personal aspect and withstand the odd tingling heat that infiltrated her every time she clashed with Nikolai's stunning dark, black-lashed eyes. It was attraction. What else could it be? And it made her hate herself.

'You wanted the chance to speak to me,' Nikolai reminded her levelly. 'I have no idea what you want to say
to me…apart from the obvious. If you're planning to
pluck the violin strings, it won't work on me. Let's cut
to the bottom line: this is business, nothing personal—'

'But it *is* personal to my family!'

'Your family is no concern of mine,' Nikolai declared with unapologetic assurance. 'But I do, as it
happens, have another option to offer you.'

Tension made Ella rise slightly on her toes. 'Another
option?' she queried breathlessly.

Nikolai gazed into those luminous green eyes and
read the hope writ large there and for some reason it
made him feel like a bastard. He crushed that foreign
sensation and irritably squashed down his conscience.
What was it about her? That air of vulnerability? Her
physical delicacy? The shocking naivety that could
persuade her to look at a stranger hoping that he was
about to play the good Samaritan? How could she still
be that trusting at her age? Sadly, he was not a soft
touch, never had been, never would be and there was
no point in even trying to pretend that he was. He didn't
get close to anyone; he didn't connect with other people. He had been that way for a very long time and he
had no plans to change his basic nature. When you let
yourself care about anyone, you got kicked in the teeth
and it had happened to him so often when he was a boy
that he had learned his lesson fast.

'There is one situation in which I would be prepared
to write off your father's debts,' he admitted.

In the unearthly silence that dragged, her tension
heightened and her tummy gave a nervous flip. 'Well,
what is that situation?' she pressed impatiently.

'You move in with me in London for a period of three months,' Nikolai outlined smoothly.

Her eyes opened wide and rounded in bewilderment. '*Move in* with you? And exactly what would that entail?'

'What it usually entails when a man and a woman live together,' Nikolai countered, wondering why he wasn't just spelling the terms out with his usual directness.

Possibly he was a little squeamish about the terms. Her reactions, the unmistakeable shyness she couldn't hide, were persuading him that, unlikely as it seemed, she might indeed be a virgin. He would very much like to take her to bed but he really didn't want her there on sufferance. He didn't particularly want to be the man who deflowered her either, although, when he thought about that aspect, he realised that he didn't want any other man to do it for him.

All of a sudden his brain was leaping about in directions he hadn't counted on, throwing up objections to what had seemed perfectly simple and straightforward only an hour before. And all that had changed was that Ella Palmer was now in front of him, and, instead of being merely a step in an ongoing project, was becoming very much a *lust* object in her own light.

Nikolai was confounded by that too because she was not his usual type. He went for tall, curvy blondes and Ella was tiny, skinny and almost as bare of curves as a teenaged boy. So, he had no understanding of precisely why he had developed a throbbing hard-on the instant a slight movement made her tiny, unfettered breasts shift below her T-shirt. Now he could see pointed nipples poking through the thin fabric and his body was eager to see a lot more of that slender but highly feminine body of hers. However, that was sex, nothing more, and he had many more convenient options in that line, didn't he? *Diavole*, why was he thinking such thoughts? What was the matter with him? He had never allowed himself to be driven by what lay south of his belt.

'You want me to be your girlfriend…?' Ella mumbled in wonderment, barely crediting that they were truly having such a conversation.

Nikolai winced. 'I don't have girlfriends… I have sex.'

'So, you're a man whore,' Ella pronounced before she could think better of it, for in her experience there were only two types of men available. One type was open to the possibility of meeting the *one* and commitment while the other type only wanted to sleep around with the maximum possible number of women.

His dark-as-jet eyes flashed like golden flames. 'Don't apply that label to me!'

'Oddly enough I wasn't trying to be insulting. I just meant that you only want sex and I know there are women like that too, so, although I shouldn't have said it, I was simply stating a fact.' Ella finally fumbled to a perspiring halt, her skin dampening below her clothing while she inwardly acknowledged the foolishness of saying anything he could find offensive. 'I'm only trying to interpret what you suggested as an option— if *not* girlfriend…?'

'Mistress,' Nikolai slotted in cool as ice.

Ella blinked, thinking he did not just say that…*did he*? Such a delightfully old-fashioned role for such a modern man. But then what did she know about Nikolai Drakos? She turned away from him, wandered over to the window and was surprised to see a big glossy dark limousine complete with driver parked outside. The limo could only belong to him, which meant that Nikolai was rich and privileged and that the concept of having a mistress to cater to his sexual needs might not seem as much of an anomaly to him as it was to her.

Unhappily, shock had welded Ella's tongue to the roof of her mouth because he was sexually propositioning her and nothing could have prepared her for that possibility. She wasn't drop-dead gorgeous…ironically, *he* was! Male heads didn't tend to swivel when Ella walked down the street because she had neither the length of leg nor the curves usually deemed necessary to attract such attention. Why on earth could he be making *her* such an offer?

'But we don't even know each other,' she framed dazedly. 'You're a stranger…'

'If you live with me I won't be a stranger for long,' Nikolai pointed out with monumental calm.

And the very sound of that inhuman calm and cool forced her to flip round and settle distraught eyes on his lean, darkly handsome face. 'You can't be serious about this!'

'I assure you that I am deadly serious. Move in and I'll forget your family's debts.'

'But it's a *crazy* idea!' She gasped, having failed to get him to acknowledge that reality and floundering against his restrained silence. It was obvious that he was determined to behave as though such a proposition were an everyday occurrence.

'It's not crazy to me,' Nikolai asserted. 'When I want anything, I go after it hard and fast.'

Her lashes dipped. Did he want her like that?

Enough to track her down, buy up her father's debts, and try and buy rights to her and her body along with those debts? The very idea of that made her dizzy and plunged her brain into even greater turmoil. 'It's immoral…it's blackmail.'

'It's definitely *not* blackmail. I'm giving you the benefit of a choice you didn't have before I came through that door,' Nikolai Drakos fielded with glittering cool. 'That choice is yours to make.'

'Like hell it is!' Ella fired back. 'The choice you're offering is totally unscrupulous.'

'When did I say I had scruples?' Nikolai asked almost conversationally. 'I want what I want and I want you in London to take out and show off.'

'But…*why*?' she interrupted, helpless in the grip of her desire to know that answer. 'Why pick me? I said no that night…was that all it took to fire you up? For you to suggest this?'

'I'm not going to answer those questions. I don't need to,' Nikolai told her without apology. 'My motivation is my own. Either you want to consider the option I've offered or you don't. It's entirely up to you.'

'But a mistress…!' A driven laugh fell from Ella's convulsing throat because she was struggling to accept that he could have confronted her with such an insane choice. 'Don't you understand that even if I wanted to say yes I couldn't?'

He frowned. 'What are you talking about?'

'My father wouldn't live with himself if he knew I was sleeping with a man just to get him out of trouble! No, the mistress option is a total impossibility as far as I am concerned.'

'That's for you to decide.' Nikolai settled a busi-

ness card down on the desk. 'My phone number. I'll
be staying at the Wrother Links Hotel until tomorrow.'

'I've already made my decision and it's a no,' Ella
hastened to tell him.

Nikolai flashed her a slow wicked smile that radi-
ated charisma. 'Think about it properly before you say
no but if you discuss it with anyone else, I'll withdraw
the offer,' he warned her smoothly. 'It's a strictly con-
fidential option.'

'You know, you can't simply ask a woman you don't
know to live with you,' she bit out, fit to be tied at his
sheer nerve and nonchalance.

Black curling lashes screening his shrewd gaze,
Nikolai shrugged a broad shoulder. 'I believe I just did.'

'But it's barbaric!' she exclaimed. 'A complete cheat
of a supposed offer!'

Nikolai sent her a gleaming sideways glance. 'No,
the real cheat was you kissing me the way you did last
year and then saying no and acting as if I had grossly
insulted you,' he murmured with lethal quietness.

'You *did* insult me!' Ella flung back, her cheeks hot
as fire while she wondered if her refusal that night had
started off his whole chain reaction. What else could
possibly be driving him?

Nikolai straightened lazily as he opened the door.
'If you take offence that easily, maybe it's just as well
that the answer is no.'

Strangely that wasn't what she wanted to hear and
she didn't understand that truth, nor the feeling that his
departure was somehow a low point rather than something to be celebrated. She watched the limo drive off,
her thoughts miles away, trailing back down the time-
line to the moment she had first met Nikolai Drakos…

* * *

Her stepmother's best friend, Ailsa, had been a wedding planner and when one of Ailsa's part-time workers had taken ill, Joy had insisted that Ella step in. Ella could have declined but she had been too well aware that if she crossed the older woman Joy would throw a tantrum and rain down misery on the whole family. And she had always hated listening to her stepmother torment her father with nasty, sneering comments. When Ella had arrived at the country house that evening she had been startled to be asked to park cars rather than wait tables as she had dimly expected. And, truth to tell, with an advanced driving test under her belt and a love of fast cars, parking the luxury models driven by the wedding guests would have been fun, had her foot not slid off the pedal of that McLaren Spider, causing the wing of it to be grazed against an overhanging bush.

Nikolai had started shouting and Ailsa had come running out to smooth over the incident. Unfortunately, Ella's immediate apology had had no effect and Ailsa had made a big deal out of supposedly sacking Ella simply to comfort Nikolai. That was when Nikolai had suddenly cooled off, dismissed the matter and insisted that he didn't want Ella sacked before striding into the house to join the rest of the guests.

It had been much later that night before she'd seen Nikolai again. She had been outside the ballroom listening to the DJ playing for the evening party while half dancing to the beat of the music to keep warm in the cold. And when she had heard something behind her, she had spun and he had simply been standing there watching her, dark eyes glowing golden as melted caramel in the reflected lights.

'If you want your car, you can fetch it for yourself,' Ella told him.

'You're right. I wouldn't allow you behind the wheel of it again,' he admitted, strolling almost soundlessly closer to gaze down at her. He had moved very quietly for such a big male. 'When do you finish tonight?'

'I'm finished now. I'm waiting for a lift home from one of the bartenders.'

'Could be a long wait,' he murmured softly.

'Could be.' Lifting her head, Ella shook her hair back from her face because the breeze was blowing it into her eyes.

'You have gorgeous hair,' he breathed.

'Thank you…' In the light flooding through the windows behind her, she could see his lean dark features with clarity and all she could think at that moment was that he was definitely the most gorgeous man she had ever come across.

'And stunning eyes…but, you're a rubbish driver.'

'My shoe slid on the pedal. I have an advanced driving test.'

'Don't believe you.'

Ella lifted her chin. 'Your problem, not mine.'

'My problem is that I want you,' Nikolai said boldly. 'I saw you dancing by the window and it gave me a high.'

Sharply disconcerted, Ella reddened. 'Oh—'

'Oh?' he mimicked with derision. 'That's it, that's all you've got to say?'

'What do you want me to say?' Ella rolled her eyes expressively. 'I'm not looking for a man right now.'

'And I'm not looking for a woman... I'm looking for *one* night,' Nikolai admitted silkily, lean brown fingers reaching up to curl into the fall of her hair and urge her closer than she would have chosen to be, had she been in her right mind.

As for that, what happened next proved to her that she was not in her right mind when Nikolai was around her because he closed his other hand to her spine and tilted her forward into sudden searing contact with his long, hard body. Within seconds he was kissing her as she had never been kissed before, forcing apart her lips with the hard pressure of his, sliding in his tongue, and sending such a jolt of wild excitement through her that her head swam and her knees buckled. He was passionate and demanding and all-male hungry, every sinuously sexual movement of his lean hips and powerful thighs against her warning her that a kiss could be almost as sizzlingly intimate as a naked embrace.

He lifted his handsome dark head and the chill of the night air on her back contrasted with the heat of his powerfully aroused body against hers. Immediately, Ella remembered who she was and where she was and the chill on her skin slivered inside right down to her stomach, and sickened her.

'Thanks, but no, thanks,' she said tartly, pulling free and starting to walk away.

'You can't be serious,' he breathed, his surprise audible because he knew she had been fired up just as much as he.

But what he didn't know was that Ella had never been that aroused...*ever*. And mere weeks after she had watched the love of her life being laid in the ground at twenty-four years of age, that truth hurt so bad that she almost sobbed over it. She had believed she truly wanted Paul but Paul had never made her feel like that and the pain of that acknowledgement tore into her grief and ate her alive with guilt.

'Watch me go,' she told Nikolai thinly, walking towards the back entrance of the country house where she would wait for her lift…regardless of how long because it would be infinitely safer than going any place with the male who had just kissed her. Kissed her until there was no yesterday and no Paul in her mind. Kissed her for now, for the moment, for a cheap pickup and one-night stand. She knew she was in a big enough emotional mess without making that mistake and doing something she would undoubtedly regret…

As she filed paperwork to tidy Rosie's desk, Ella drifted back from that powerful memory and shivered. She had blown him off. Even though it hadn't been intentional, she had given him the impression that she was with him every step of the way during that kiss and then she had changed her mind. But a woman was entitled to change her mind and she had exercised that right. Yet had she become that much more desirable after she walked away? How many women had said no to Nikolai? Ella reckoned that score would be low because he was very handsome and evidently wealthy into the bargain. Nikolai was a hard hitter, an achiever. Had she challenged his male ego?

Was it really pure coincidence that he now owned her father's debts? He hadn't answered her questions. He had said he was giving her a choice she hadn't had before he arrived, and, although she didn't like to see it that way, she saw that it was the unwelcome truth.

The father and grandmother she adored were on the brink of losing everything they had left. How could she stand back and let them suffer when she had been given an alternative?

Throughout the day her mind seethed with wild ideas. She was willing to do just about anything to save the roof over her family's head. Freed from the burden of those awful debts and Joy's extravagance, her father would finally be in a position to make a reasonable living again. Although he had lost the furniture shop, he remained a qualified accountant and the ability to work again would give him his self-respect back.

Yet while Ella might want to help her family, Nikolai Drakos had put her in an impossible situation. Her father would never accept such a sacrifice on her part. So, how could she get around that obvious stumbling block?

Well, one possibility would be offering Nikolai the intimate night she suspected he felt cheated out of. She shuddered at the prospect of having sex with anyone in such circumstances but just as quickly told herself off for being a drama queen. Why make a three-act tragedy out of a perfectly normal feature of life? If possessing her body meant that much to the man, he was welcome to it.

It was not as though she were still a virgin because she had actively chosen to embrace that state. She had waited for Paul, for the miraculous day when he would be 'well enough', only that opportunity had failed to arrive. Now and not for the first time she wished Paul had not been so exacting in his wishes, so determined that everything be right and perfect before they became intimate, because going to bed with Nikolai would have been much less intimidating had Ella already acquired some sexual experience. One night, she told herself bleakly, yes, she could do one night if it saved her family. Were there any other options?

Well, instead of making her a mistress, Nikolai could *marry* her, lending their entire arrangement the sort of respectable patina that would allow her father to accept his debts being paid off, because a son-in-law was a family member while a lover who was a stranger was something else entirely. Somehow she didn't think Nikolai would want to go for the wedding-ring option. In fact a reluctant giggle was forced from between Ella's tense lips at even the idea of making such a suggestion. The man who didn't date and only had sex was unlikely to warm to the prospect of holy matrimony...

At the end of her working day, Ella called the number on the business card Nikolai had left her and before he could even speak said, 'I want to come and see you this evening.'

Taken aback by that bold declaration, Nikolai frowned. 'You've changed your mind?'

'I want to talk...'

Nikolai was dubious. He had already wondered how sure she was of Cyrus's support if she was willing to turn *his* offer down without hesitation. Had his old enemy already proposed to her? Yet wouldn't she have thrown that information at him?

'There's nothing to *talk* about,' he countered.

'Where there's a will, there's a way,' Ella quoted Gramma in her desperation to get him to listen.

Ten minutes later, Ella walked into the exclusive Wrother Links Hotel. Rather belatedly she became conscious of her shabby work clothing, which consisted of

a tee and worn skinny jeans thrust into sensible ankle
boots. Perhaps she should have gone home first and
changed and used some make-up, she reflected uneasily. But then Nikolai had outlined his outrageous
proposal at the start of her working day when she was
looking far from glamorous. Her smooth brow indented.

What did the wretched man want from her?

The obvious, she told herself irritably as the re-
ceptionist directed her into the lift with a curious appraisal. Just because she had never viewed her body
as a means of negotiation didn't mean Nikolai felt the
same. He had to want her for something and her body
was the most likely explanation, Ella reasoned uncomfortably. Over the years she had listened to friends in-
sist that men saw sex as being of crucial importance,
which had left her confused, dealing with Paul's rigid
self-discipline.

Even so, it was an enormous challenge for Ella to
credit that suave, sophisticated Nikolai Drakos could
possibly see a woman like her in some irresistible had-
to-possess-her light. When she had first gone to uni to
study, she had been bombarded by sexual approaches.
In many ways that was why meeting Paul, initially only
a friend, had been such a relief. Paul had valued her
for the person she was, not for her body or the physical
pleasure he assumed she could give him. Paul, however, had been a very special case, she reminded herself with regret.

A young man who introduced himself as Nikolai's
employee opened the door of the suite and ushered her
in. The desk in the room was scattered with papers, a
laptop sitting open on it. She got a glance at the col-

umns of figures on the screen before the employee closed it down and gathered the papers into a file to take his leave.

'Mr Drakos will be with you shortly,' he assured her as he departed.

Ella stared out of the window at the renowned golf course and, in an effort to steady her leaping nerves when she heard a sound somewhere behind her, she said, 'Do you play golf?'

'No. Not my game,' Nikolai proclaimed as he shook out his shirt. 'Why are you here, Ella?'

Ella spun round and focused in consternation on Nikolai's incredibly well-defined muscular abs and stomach as he pulled on a shirt. Clearly he was fresh from the shower with his black hair still curling damply and his hard-boned jaw clean-shaven, but the bronzed expanse of naked male flesh on show above the belt encircling his lean hips sharply disconcerted her. Cheeks warming, she glanced away. 'Is it inconvenient?'

'Let's call it unexpected,' he replied, his brilliant dark eyes resting on her.

Well, there was nothing of the seductress in her appearance, Nikolai acknowledged wryly. He had assumed she would dress up but she hadn't made the effort, which for some strange reason irritated him. Wasn't he worth that much effort? In the shower he had reminded himself that approaching Ella Palmer had always been a long shot. After all, if she had already had one rich man in the palm of her hand why would she accept another dictating terms to her? And yet the fact remained that, astonishingly, Cyrus was evidently not coming to his supposed future wife's rescue and had taken himself off on a long trip to China. Maybe the tip-off Nikolai had received about Cyrus's marital plans was rubbish, maybe Cyrus was simply playing with Ella…as he did in the initial stages of his games with such women, when he played the honourable respectful male to perfection to lull any suspicion of his true intentions.

'The unexpected doesn't always have to be bad,' Ella fenced while he buttoned his shirt. Her cheeks were hot because the little peepshow he had unthinkingly subjected her to had made perspiration break out on her skin below clothes that suddenly felt too tight and constricting.

'I believe you're acquainted with Cyrus Makris,' he remarked.

Startled, Ella glanced at him. 'Yes. He's a family friend. I was engaged to his nephew, Paul, until he died,' she told him, wondering how he had known about her acquaintance with Cyrus before a vague association occurred to her. 'Your name… I should've guessed. You're Greek as well, aren't you?'

'I am. Would you like a drink?'

'No, thanks.' Ella simply wanted to get what she had to say said and then run. 'Can't stay long anyway. I left my dog outside in the van.'

'So…?' Nikolai prompted, watching a strand of bronze hair fan out across her white throat as she lifted her head high, her pale skin accentuating the luminous green of her eyes and the succulent pink of her lips. He tensed, fighting the incipient throb at his groin with annoyance.

'Would…?' Ella breathed in deep and straightened her spine. 'I'm here to ask if one night would do.'

'One night of what?' Nikolai queried blankly.

'You know, sex, for goodness' sake!' Ella launched back at him in furious embarrassment. 'I mean, if that's all you want, I hardly need to go to London and live with you for it!'

Nikolai surveyed her in shock and it took a great deal to shock him. 'Let me get this straight…you're offering me a night of sex instead?'

'Don't make it sound so sordid!' Ella lashed back at him.

'It wasn't me who made the offer. No, the night of sex wouldn't meet my…requirements.' Nikolai selected the word and voiced it smooth as silk. 'I also assume by that offer that you're not a virgin?'

'And why would you think I was at my age?' But Ella thought better of lying because there was always the hope that the truth would be a total turn-off for him. 'Actually, I am inexperienced but…'

Distaste at the entire conversation was filling Nikolai. Of course she had assumed he wanted her for sex. What else was she supposed to think? But he wasn't a ball of sleaze like Cyrus, who treated women like toys he enjoyed breaking. And as it occurred to Nikolai what a challenge making that offer must have been for an innocent like her, he almost swore and had to fight back an angry sense of discomfiture. For the very first time he appreciated that he had recklessly plunged himself into a scenario that was not at all his style.

'One night won't work for me,' Nikolai admitted in a driven undertone.

Ella's heart was thumping at what felt like a mile a minute behind her breastbone. Relief and dismay assailed her in equal parts. Naturally she was very relieved not to be asked to immediately deliver on the shameless proposition she had just made, but she was taken aback by the speed and power of his repudiation as well. What did he really want? What on earth more could he possibly want or expect from her?

'Then I only have one other…suggestion to make,' she murmured tightly. 'You marry me.'

'*Marry* you?' Nikolai exclaimed after an unnervingly protracted pause while he studied her with incredulous force. 'Are you out of your mind?'

She had finally got an honest and true reaction out of Nikolai Drakos, Ella realised, and a curious feeling of triumph mingled with her mortification. The idea of getting married had shattered him, scoring colour along those amazing high cheekbones, widening his stunning dark-fringed golden eyes. Evidently he had not been prepared for that idea.

CHAPTER THREE

'IT WAS A purely practical suggestion from my point of view,' Ella told him curtly.

'You need to change your point of view,' Nikolai retorted with sardonic bite.

Her face was burning with embarrassment and her hands had closed into tight little fists of restraint. If he couldn't be more frank about exactly what he needed from her, then he could take the rough with the smooth and it would be his own fault. 'I can't. You would have to marry me to persuade my father that it was acceptable for you to write off his debts. He's no freeloader.'

'There is no way that I will marry you to get what I want!' Nikolai cut in with a raw edge of impatience to his dark deep drawl.

'Then that concludes our discussion,' Ella stated without heat, simply desperate to escape the opulent hotel suite and forget that she had ever met him. As her father had said when he had put the family home on the line and lost it, well, at least he knew he had tried. Well, she now knew what it was like to try hard and still fail too.

'*Diavole*, Ella!' Nikolai bit out as she reached the door. 'There *has* to be another way!'

Ella spun round. 'No, there honestly isn't. My father couldn't live with the idea that his daughter would move in with some man to clear his debts.'

His melted caramel eyes suddenly flashed as brilliant a gold as sunlight. 'You have the rare ability to make everything sound sleazy!'

'No, you just don't like plain speaking...unless it's you doing it. And you talk in riddles. You asked me to be your mistress yet you say no to the chance to sleep with me.'

'Obviously I want more from you than sex. I can get sex anywhere, any time,' he assured her dismissively.

Frustration roared through Ella. 'I'm not a secret heiress, am I?'

'What the hell are you talking about?'

'I thought I might be the sixth cousin of some distant relation who's worth a fortune and that you had found out and that maybe—'

'Your imagination is more inventive than mine. But in that situation a man would want marriage to secure his share of the inheritance. However, in *this* instance...' Nikolai compressed his wide sensual mouth.

Marriage, even a fake marriage, was out of the question. Nikolai had never wanted to get married. From the little he remembered of his irresponsible parents, they had fought continually and spent their money on alcohol and drugs while neglecting their two children. He probably wouldn't have survived early childhood without the loving care of his older sister, who had had a real live baby to look after instead of a doll. No, Nikolai would be perfectly happy to leave the world without descendants of his own. Nor could he imagine wanting one woman for the rest of his life and shun-

ning all others. He barely repressed a shudder because
he set a high value on his freedom of choice.

'In this instance?' Ella prompted.

'I need you with me in London.'

'But as I've already explained, you can't have me
without a wedding ring. You know, I don't want to
marry you either,' Ella admitted shortly. 'But if it
makes my family happy and secure again, I would do
it for their sake.'

'I wouldn't even consider it. *I* will deal with your
family,' Nikolai said flatly.

'What on earth do you mean?'

What it really came down to was how far he was
prepared to go in his efforts to punish Cyrus, Nikolai reflected. A fleeting image of his sister's gentle
smile, brought to the surface by memories of his background, froze him in place. There should be and there
would be *no* limits to his desire for revenge. If others
got caught up in the backlash, what was that to him?
He could not afford to have a conscience. Ella was a
pawn, nothing more.

'I will tell your family that we've been seeing each
other and that now we want to be together in London,'
Nikolai explained smoothly. 'Your father cannot struggle to settle debts that no longer exist. He will not have
the luxury of choice.'

'You think it's a luxury for me to be able to *choose*
to be your mistress?' Ella launched at him furiously,
rage bubbling up through her slight body like a hot
spring at the prospect of that indignity. 'But I've already said no to that option!'

'Which is wasting my time and your own! You can't
renegotiate the terms just because you don't like them.

I won't let you. There will be no single night, no marriage either,' he asserted in a harsh undertone, his lean, darkly handsome features forbidding in cast, his stunning eyes hard as black diamonds. 'Either you come to London to be with me or I walk away. That's the *only* choice you have!'

The raw tension straining the atmosphere sent a wave of dizziness through Ella. Consternation brought her defensive barriers crashing down. He had ruthlessly rejected her options. Her head swimming a little, she closed her hands over the back of a tall chair to force her body to stand steady. She stared back at him with a sinking heart. It was the moment she had been fighting to avoid since he'd first confronted her earlier that day. The 'grit your teeth and deal' moment when there was no room left to wriggle. Perspiration dampened her skin.

'Your sole source of interest here should be the pay-off,' Nikolai reminded her drily. 'And learning to do as you are told.'

In the rushing silence, Ella wrinkled her nose. 'If I don't agree with something, I'm hopeless at doing what I'm told.'

'But you can learn,' Nikolai sliced in, his tone as glacial as ice water. 'Don't sign up for this if you can't respect the rules.'

'Perhaps you could tell me how I'm supposed to respect a man who wants me even though I don't want him?' Ella shot back at him in scornful challenge.

'Do you always lie in preference to telling the truth about yourself?' Nikolai enquired dangerously softly as he strode closer.

Ella found herself backed up against the door before

she could grab the opportunity to make the swift exit
she had originally planned. 'I'm not lying—'

Nikolai rested the palm of one hand against the door
and gazed down at her with hard dark eyes. 'The worst
of it is that you know you're lying…but I don't play
that game.'

'I want to leave.'

'Not until I say you can,' Nikolai fenced, so big he
was like a wall blocking the rest of the room from her
view and cutting out most of the light, so that for the
first time she wished she were wearing heels to cut the
ridiculous height differential between them to a more
reasonable level.

Ella turned up her face, chin tilted at an obstinate
angle, green eyes sparkling. 'I could use my knee to
persuade you.'

'Why would you damage a part of me you hope to
enjoy?' Nikolai countered.

'It would take an avalanche to crush your ego,
wouldn't it?'

'If I was modest you would walk all over me with
pleasure.' Nikolai was entranced by the glorious green
of her eyes against the smooth, fine grain of her porcelain skin. 'But that's not what you want from me, is
it? You'd much prefer me to take your choices away
and give you the excuse to *be* with me.'

'That's rubbish!' Ella gasped, barely able to credit
that he had made such an allegation. 'I don't want or
need an excuse to be with you!'

'*Ne*…yes, you do,' Nikolai insisted, pinning her up
against the door in blatant entrapment. 'You want excuses and persuasion and, sadly, you're not going to
get them from me. That's not how I am with a woman.'

'Fascinating as this dialogue no doubt is to a man who likes to listen to the sound of his own voice, I'm not interested.'

'Every time you lie to me I'll punish you.'

'Punish me?' Ella parroted, blinking in bewilderment.

Nikolai bent down and scooped her up, disconcerted by how very light she was. Yes, she was small and slight in build but he was convinced she weighed too little to be healthy. Nikolai walked through the room into the bedroom with her in his arms. 'You'll like the way I punish you.'

'What are you doing?' Ella exclaimed as he swept her off her feet.

'Sealing our agreement.'

'What agreement?' she demanded rawly as he dropped her down on a bed so well sprung that she bounced.

'Your agreement to be my mistress.' He savoured the word.

As Ella made a sudden sidewise motion intended to remove her from the bed Nikolai came down and imprisoned her with the vastly superior weight and strength of his big, powerful body. 'Get off me. Let go of me…*right now*!' she raked at him.

'I really hate being shouted at,' Nikolai confided a split second before his hard, sensual mouth claimed hers.

And for that same split second it was as though Ella's world stopped turning and she was jolted off course, sent breathless and spinning into the unknown. Heat surged up through her like an invasive weapon. He eased her out from under him but kept her trapped in his arms. Irritation flamed through her because inexplicably she had liked his crushing weight on hers. Her fists struck at shirt-clad shoulders as unyielding as rock. The tip of his tongue flicked inside her mouth and she shivered violently, the clenching at her secret core almost painful in its intensity. He nipped at her lower lip, sucked and soothed it with his tongue. She wanted more, she wanted more so badly it hurt to be denied and the rushing tide of that hunger shocked her back into her mind again.

His kisses were like nothing she'd ever experienced before. A lean hand tunnelled below her tee and closed round a small, high breast, long fingers stroking the throbbing tip and lingering to rub and tug until her spine arched in response and her hips jerked up and a helpless sound of craving was released from low in her throat.

He pushed up the T-shirt and replaced his fingers with his mouth. She was so sensitive there that she quivered beneath every lash of his tongue, every teasing brush of his teeth, and the molten heat pulsing between her thighs was swelling and swelling in an unstoppable rise. Her hips shifted, the driving need for relief powering her every instinctive movement, and then the surge at the heart of her became so urgent, so utterly overpowering that a jagged climax took her by storm. The wave of excitement that jerked her in his hold left her sobbing for breath and mental clarity as shock seized hold of her instead.

In a driven movement that took him by surprise, Ella rolled off the bed and yanked down her T-shirt with shaking hands. Her face was hot as a fire and her entire body was throbbing and trembling in the backwash of an orgasm more powerful than anything she had ever experienced. Her nerves were shot to hell. She couldn't even breathe normally. Momentarily she closed her eyes tight, praying for self-control. He could make her want him. He touched her, he kissed her and everything, including her proud protest of indifference, went haywire. Her body raged wildly out of control around him, which was just one more reason for her to hate him.

Dry-mouthed, Nikolai studied her, fighting his raging libido. He literally *ached*. He wanted to haul her back to the bed and pin her under him to drive into the hot, sweet release of her tiny body, and the intensity of his desire sent a chill of recoil snaking through him. He didn't do intense in any form. He didn't get excited about sex. He didn't do exclusive. He steered clear of entanglements and complications. Revenge and work motivated him. He had never *needed* anything else. He had never needed a woman and, if he had anything to do with it, he never would.

'I'm leaving,' she told him flatly while she fought harder than she ever had in her life to rescue some kind of composure. After quivers of reaction were still travelling through her treacherous body, while she tried not to question her total loss of control, keen not to think along such demeaning lines in his presence.

Nikolai sprang off the bed, shoving his shirt back below his belt. 'I'll follow you back.'

'Follow me *where*? What are you planning to do?'

'Ease your move to London.'

'Don't you dare go near my family!' Ella warned him furiously. 'You're a stranger to them.'

'But I won't be a stranger for long,' Nikolai asserted, picking up a jacket.

'You don't know what you're doing. They're not stupid. They're never going to believe that I've been seeing some man in secret!' she told him with scorn.

Nikolai elevated a fine black brow. 'People believe what they want to believe and they'll be relieved that you've started living again.'

Ella's face shuttered. 'I don't know what you're talking about.'

'I'm not stupid either. You're a woman and most women are dramatic. I bet you swore you'd never love again after your fiancé died. I bet you've hugged your grief to you like a security blanket ever since,' Nikolai opined.

Ella had turned white as bone. She flung him a look of loathing. 'How dare you drag Paul into this? How do you even know about him?'

'I know enough about you to make an educated guess or two,' Nikolai drawled coolly.

'Well, you got it wrong, badly wrong,' she assured him, but she was lying because although she would never have admitted it he had got it all frighteningly right. In fact his accuracy was both uncanny and mortifying. She *had* sworn that she would never love again, that she would never date another man after Paul. Her grief had been so great that she had voiced bitter self-destructive sentiments that had contained little common sense. The last thing she needed to hear now was Nikolai Drakos implying that she had acted like a drama queen craving sympathy and attention.

'So, quite naturally, your family will be delighted to believe that you have moved on after your loss and their pleasure in that reality will help them gloss over any inconsistencies in our story. They will *want* us to be real,' Nikolai declared with a sardonic smile. 'Your only role is to act happy about moving to London to see more of me.'

Something akin to panic assailed Ella's breathing process, tightening her chest, closing her throat. Act happy? She wasn't sure she knew how to do that. Life had been too challenging in recent years to offer many such opportunities but she had learned to smile and fake it for her family's benefit. No, it was the idea of moving to London and an unfamiliar environment to *be* with Nikolai that shocked and dismayed her most. And the concept of living with a man, being *intimate* with a man like Nikolai Drakos utterly unnerved her. Yet if she didn't agree to Nikolai's demands her family's life would be ruined. And after the setbacks and upheavals her father and Gramma had already lived through, how could they possibly cope with more at their age?

Almost three hours later, Ella let Gramma herd her into the kitchen for a private chat. She went reluctantly because she was straining to eavesdrop on the conversation that Nikolai was having with her father in the dining room the older man had long used as an office. The men's voices rose and fell, Nikolai's deep-pitched drawl soothing the rising note in her father's audible objections.

'I want Ella happy and she won't be happy if she's worrying herself sick about her family back home,' Nikolai asserted forcefully.

Ella paled. Nikolai would be saying all the right things and wearing all the right expressions, she reflected bitterly. He was clearly a consummate liar and smooth as molasses in a situation that would have sent nine out of ten men running for the hills. In action he was a breathtakingly quick study. He had arrived just after the family finished dinner and joined them for tea and carrot cake. He had grasped Ella's hand to declare that they had been seeing each other for months, ever since they had met the night she was parking cars. He had been very convincing, very persuasive and she had little doubt that he would soon crush her father's protests and persuade him to accept that his debts were being written off.

'Do you know what surprised me most about all this? Nikolai is *so* different from Paul,' Gramma remarked as Ella began to load the dishwasher to keep her restive hands busy. 'He's a real man's man.'

Ella's soft mouth compressed. The older woman had a traditional outlook. She liked men who could hunt a wild boar before breakfast and reduce a pile of logs to wood chips by dinner time. Paul's lack of interest in traditional male pursuits had bemused Gramma. She had liked him and treated him like a son but she had never understood him, Ella conceded with regret.

'I never thought that you would go for someone like Nikolai. Of course, he's very good-looking and obviously successful. Are you sure you know what you're getting into with him?' the older woman pressed. 'I know living together is very popular these days but I noticed that there was no talk of an engagement in the future or anything like that.'

'Let's see how it goes first. We may be too different. It may not work out between us,' Ella commented, dropping the first hint towards her eventual breakup with Nikolai. 'Who can tell when we haven't been able to spend much time together here?'

'Why didn't you tell us about him?' Gramma demanded for at least the third time. 'Are we so unapproachable?'

'I said a lot of stupid stuff after Paul died,' Ella muttered numbly.

'You were hurt, grieving. It was normal for you to feel that way,' Gramma assured her. 'I only want to be sure you're not leaping into this too fast with Nikolai. You're turning your whole life upside down for him. I did like the fact though that he said you might choose to pick up and continue your veterinary training again.'

Yes, if there were any right impressive things to say, Nikolai had contrived to corner the market on those sentiments, Ella ruminated bitterly. He came, he saw, he conquered. Her father and her grandmother had sat in awe while Nikolai shared his supposed thoughts. Acting as though he loved her had come so very naturally to him that it had spooked Ella. He had never said the words, but his behaviour had convinced his receptive audience that he cared deeply for Ella and only wanted her happiness.

'He's what you need,' the older woman murmured. 'A fresh start somewhere new. However, I suspect that this development is going to come as a huge shock to Cyrus.'

'I expect so,' Ella remarked uncertainly, thinking that it had come as a huge shock to her as well, although she could hardly admit the fact.

'You haven't a suspicion, have you?' Gramma grimaced. 'I don't think Cyrus sees you only as Paul's former fiancée. In fact I believe his interest is a lot more personal.'

Ella studied her grandmother's troubled face in consternation and winced. 'No, you're totally wrong about that. What on earth gave you such a *horrible* idea?'

'It *would* be horrible to you, then…' The older woman gathered with a hint of relief. 'For a while I was a bit worried that his attentions might be welcome?'

'There hasn't been any attentions,' Ella contradicted defensively.

'The flowers…the lunch dates…that big charity do…him asking you to check his house while he's away.'

'For a start, Cyrus has only sent me flowers a couple of times and the charity thing was a special favour. There's only been a couple of lunch dates and those were only casual catch-ups,' Ella protested. 'And me calling in to check his house when he has a resident housekeeper was just Cyrus being plain silly! I think he got all riled up about that spate of country-house robberies last year. Honestly, Gramma, Cyrus has never done or said anything that would give me the idea that he sees me as anything other than his late nephew's fiancée and a family friend.'

'Well, I think you've missed the signs. I don't like the way he looks at you and I wouldn't let your father approach him for a loan because I was worried it might come with strings attached,' Gramma confided uncomfortably.

Had Ella been in the mood to laugh, she would have laughed then at the irony of her grandmother's misgivings. Evidently the older woman had misread Cyrus's motives and distrusted him but she had offered Nikolai and his honeyed hollow lies a red-carpet welcome.

'Ella…?' Nikolai called her from the hall.

Grudgingly she went to the doorway. Butch pushed

out past her to caper round Nikolai's feet. From the instant of first laying eyes on Nikolai the tiny dog had been inexplicably smitten and craving his attention.

'Show me out. I need to get back to the hotel and start organising everything. That animal is insane,' he breathed, stepping carefully to avoid his canine companion.

'What do you have to organise?' Ella queried, shooing her pet away while wondering why Butch wasn't picking up on her hostility towards his new idol.

'Arrangements for your move,' Nikolai advanced, pulling open the front door with a lean, powerful hand and stepping out into the cool evening air.

As Ella closed the door in the little dog's face he began to fuss and bark in annoyance. 'You think you've won, don't you?' she whispered bitterly as soon as she was free from the risk of being overheard by her family.

Nikolai swung round, dark golden eyes as bright as torches, a satisfied half-smile lifting his sardonic mouth. 'I *know* I've won and you should be pleased. Everyone's happy.'

'Everyone but me,' Ella cut in curtly.

'I'll make you happy. You'll have fabulous clothes and fabulous jewellery,' Nikolai assured her, one hand splayed across her spine to hold her still in front of him as he lounged back against the wing of his spectacular sports car.

Ella bristled like a cat stroked the wrong way, scorn lightening her bright green eyes to palest jade. 'Those things aren't going to make me happy.'

'What about the even more fabulous sex?' Nikolai husked, both arms locking her into place in front of him, his keen gaze watching the rise of colour in her cheeks.

He couldn't stop touching her. He couldn't stop noticing things about her either. It was as though he went into supercharged observation mode in her presence. She was blushing and for some reason he revelled in having that effect on her even while he was continually surprised at the level of her innocence. How could she have been engaged and yet remain so naïve? True, the fiancé had been ill but the couple had been together for years. It must've been quite a particular relationship, he reflected in sincere puzzlement.

After all, Ella seethed with so much outright passion. At the hotel she had flared from a spark into a wild hot flame in his arms and her fiery generous response had been incredibly exciting. Indeed it was years since Nikolai had found *any* aspect of sex exciting. On a scale of one to ten his hunger for Ella had now veered into the seriously uncomfortable zone. The image of her lying against him quivering and gasping with release, her languorous green eyes pinned to him, would stay with him for ever. He didn't think he had ever wanted a woman so much and that seriously bothered him. Did it bother him enough to stop the whole scheme in its tracks?

He was promising her fabulous sex. Of course he was, Ella reflected in exasperation. Nikolai was incredibly confident of his own abilities. And maybe there was some excuse for that, she conceded as her body leant forward seemingly of its own volition, drawn by the heat and dominance of his sizzling sexual charisma.

Nikolai bent his head and kissed her. It was a slow claiming as the tip of his tongue traced the lush fullness of her lower lip and then delved gently between. A breathy little gasp erupted from her parted lips and she stepped closer. His arms snapped round her and it was the work of a moment for him to swing round and press her back against the car, his sensual mouth driving down hard on hers, his lean, powerful body crushing her against the unyielding metal.

Her every skin cell seemed to erupt into life as heat raced through her bloodstream and a bolt of naked yearning surged from low in her pelvis. His mouth was all she cared about. She couldn't get enough of him, was convinced she would never get enough of him. She gloried in the thrust of his arousal against her, the knowledge that Nikolai Drakos wanted her and couldn't hide the fact.

I want this man, she acknowledged, shocking herself rigid. Not someone she loved or respected or even liked. He exerted a primitive pull on her senses, which she could only compare to an utterly mindless desire to put her hand in a fire. But was it so destructive? So *wrong*? Wasn't it normal, even natural, that the physical side of her nature, which she had long been forced to suppress, should finally demand expression? And Nikolai was magnificent...

Nikolai wrenched himself free of her, breathing hard. She made him feel like a teenager with his first girl. It unnerved him and made the equivalent of defensive barriers of iron bars spring up inside him to police his very thought and reaction. She knocked him off balance, tore his control to shreds and he hated it. 'I'll be in touch,' he said without any expression at all.

Ella backed on hollow legs to the doorstep and watched him drive off. He had behaved as if nothing had happened. The hard, high planes of his lean dark features had betrayed no emotion. His eyes had been veiled by those ridiculously long lashes of his and his voice had been cool in tone. So where did that leave her?

Set on the road to making the biggest mistake of her life? Or to making the biggest discovery? She would make that choice, Ella promised herself squarely, *not* him. Wanting him wasn't going to make a fool out of her. She was bright enough to see that what he made her feel had nothing to do with love and caring. She wouldn't let him hurt her. She wouldn't let him use her. If there was any using to be done, *she* would be the user. And if he thought otherwise, he was in for a very big surprise…

CHAPTER FOUR

ELLA HAD TO smother a yawn while her nails were being done because she was bored stiff. A car had collected her and Butch early that morning and ferried them down to London. Parting from her father and grandmother had been tough but the knowledge that the family home was now safe and that her father was already making cheerful plans to open up a home office to work as an accountant had soothed her nerves. She had done the right thing, she was *doing* the right thing, she told herself urgently.

As soon as she had arrived in London it had been clear that her entire day had already been mapped out for her. Ella had been dropped off first while Butch and her luggage had travelled on to the town house where she would apparently be staying.

It was hours since she had arrived at the exclusive beauty salon where she had been waited on hand and foot, wrapped in fleecy towels and generally treated like an animated doll to be beautified. So far there was not one part of her that had not come in for some form of improving attention. She had been waxed and moisturised and polished to perfection. Her hair had been washed and conditioned and trimmed and now fell in silky waves round her shoulders.

In his office across the city, Nikolai couldn't concentrate. She was within reach, in *his* home. He had never lived in his late grandfather's house, however, and Ella would pretty much live there alone because Nikolai had no intention of giving up the privacy of his apartment. But his plan was coming to fruition. This very evening, Cyrus Makris would be back in London to attend the annual dinner being held to raise funds for Nikolai's favourite charity. Cyrus was, of course, a generous benefactor. He always made a point of giving money to organisations that took care of the victims of abuse. His good reputation was of unparalleled importance to him and invariably his first line of defence. But whatever else he got, he wasn't getting Ella, Nikolai reflected exultantly.

An older man wearing a bow tie and a smart black jacket opened the front door of the imposing town house. 'Miss Palmer…please come in. I'm Max, Mr Drakos's steward. I look after everything here.'

Ella walked into a surprisingly dark and ornate hall and looked around in surprise. She had somehow assumed that Nikolai would live in a very contemporary setting. But as she glanced into a massive, equally dark reception room and rolled her eyes at the clutter on every surface, she could see that indoors the clock of time had reset to the late Victorian Gothic era of interior decoration.

'My late employer, Mr Drakos's grandfather, didn't like change. This was originally his wife's family home and he kept everything the way it was after his wife passed. He got very annoyed if I moved anything.'

'My goodness; with all this stuff, how did he even notice something had been moved?' Ella exclaimed, spinning round to gape at her surroundings.

'Like the present Mr Drakos, he was a very clever and very observant man,' Max told her. 'Let me show you to your room.'

'Where's Butch…er…my dog?' Ella asked.

Max led her silently into a room with a tiled floor and a log burner. A scruffy terrier with flyaway ears lay sprawled across a rug there with Butch nestled against her. She was about twice Butch's size but Ella's pet showed no fear of the other animal. 'Good grief,' Ella framed as Butch leapt up and charged at her, his little eyes bright with welcome. His companion slowly sat up, voiced a half-hearted gruff bark before dropping her head down again, her attention welded to Butch.

'That's Mr Drakos's dog, Rory. Officially she's called Aurora. Rory took an immediate liking to Butch and has been cuddled up to him ever since. I expect she's enjoying the company.'

'I didn't know Mr Drakos had a pet.'

'She travels a lot with my employer. I'll show you upstairs now.' Max led the way up the elegant staircase.

The bed in the spacious bedroom was new, she was relieved to note, but the elaborate ebonised furniture followed the same theme as the ground-floor décor. Max opened a door to show off a high-tech en suite and she smiled. 'That must be a recent improvement.'

'When the electric and plumbing were being renewed Mr Drakos took the opportunity to install bathrooms and replace the kitchen. The redecoration project is awaiting the attention of the new mistress of the house,' Max remarked, flicking her a conspiratorial sidewise glance that made her stiffen as comprehension set in.

Seemingly the older man had misinterpreted her role in Nikolai's life and had assumed she was destined to be a wife, who would eventually take charge of the household. That was so far from the truth that it pained Ella like a nagging toothache. Max brought up her luggage and then reappeared with a beautiful long dress sheathed in a protective covering, other packaged items and several jewel boxes.

'Deliveries from Mr Drakos,' he announced. 'He phoned to say that he would collect you at seven.'

Ella raised a brow and said nothing.

Unfurling her phone, she called Nikolai when Max had left the room. 'It's Ella. Are we going out tonight?'

'Yes, I'm taking you to a gala dinner. I sent a dress, accessories and jewellery for you to wear. Haven't you received them yet? Didn't Max mention my call?'

'Yes…and yes. But you should've informed me in person.'

Nikolai compressed his hard, sensual mouth. This was why he didn't do relationships with women. He didn't want the petty squabbles, the clingy expectations or the too easy taking of offence to disrupt his day. 'I'm very busy,' he told her honestly.

'Since when have you been buying me clothes?'

'This is your new life, Ella. There'll be big changes. Get used to it.'

Seething at his stubborn, uncompromising stance, Ella ended the call. She unzipped the garment bag to reveal a designer gown. Although sleeveless and conservative in style, it was composed of the most beautiful white fabric overlaid with a shimmer of gold that glistened in the light. It was what Ella would have described as a dress fit for a princess and she was a little surprised it wasn't pink in colour and very puffy in shape. Was this what mistresses were wearing this season? Surely something sleek and black with a plunging neckline would have been more appropriate? Then it occurred to her that she had very little to show off in a plunging neckline and she squirmed.

Her cheeks fired up at the acknowledgement that she *had* agreed to be Nikolai's mistress. She studied the low, wide bed with its pristine white bedding and groaned out loud. Indecision was tearing her in two. Suddenly she felt as if she didn't know herself any more because one half of her was beyond excited at the prospect of sharing that bed with Nikolai while the other half of her was shocked and panicky. Which of those halves was her true self? In that instant she felt plunged into emotional turmoil.

Could she do it? Have meaningless sex without making a fuss about it? She wanted him, didn't she? The tightness in her chest eased at the acceptance of that fact, which made her feel more in control. Nikolai had forced a hard choice on her but what she made of the next step was solely her department. And if she was about to officially become a mistress there wasn't much point in slinking about as though she were ashamed of herself. Her family was secure again and she was grateful for the fact. She would use Nikolai for experience. The giving wasn't going to be all one-sided, she told herself firmly. She would be benefitting from his expertise. She wouldn't let herself feel anything for him either, anything *at all*. When it was over she would walk back into her own life and take it up again. That was why it was so important that she return to her veterinary training and complete it, she thought ruefully. Her career would give her a firm foundation on which to build a fresh future and it would provide her with a focus as nothing else could.

In the midst of that thought she flipped open one of the jewellery boxes and blinked in amazement at the flash of an extravagant emerald and diamond pendant. Evidently Nikolai wanted to display her like an expensive trophy, a rich man's toy. But why? She had assumed that for him it was all about sex, but now, instead of trying to take immediate advantage, he was marching her out to some formal public event. That didn't make sense. *He* didn't make sense. Nothing he did made sense. Why on earth had he settled on her in the first place?

Simply because she was free and available at the right time for a price he was willing to pay? Or because he had really, *really* wanted her last year and would do just about anything to have her? A surprising sparkle lightened her troubled gaze. She knew which option she preferred. Nikolai's proposition, his sheer, unscrupulous determination to get her into bed at any cost, was strangely flattering to a woman whose fiancé had resisted her supposed attractions at every turn.

As she went for a shower her eyes stung and misted with tears on that wounding thought.

'It doesn't have to be perfect,' she had told Paul once. 'I mean, I know it's not going to be perfect the first time. I'm not stupid. But perfect doesn't matter to me.'

Unfortunately it had evidently mattered a great deal to Paul. Yet sex wouldn't be any more perfect with Nikolai, she reasoned ruefully before sensibly shutting down her memories. Nikolai wouldn't expect perfect and something told her that he would take imperfect in his stride. He was complex but adaptable and she would have said he was less hung up on image had he not selected a dress and jewellery for her and ensured that she spent the day having her appearance tuned up at a beauty salon. Nikolai wanted her to look the very best she could and why shouldn't he?

Nikolai stilled in the hall as Ella descended the stairs with the caution of a woman wearing very high heels. The chandelier high above her head glittered over her metallic-bronze hair, picking out the deep auburn and gold strands and enhancing the radiance of her skin. The gown lengthened and shaped her tiny frame and the emerald pendant and earrings threw her luminous green eyes into striking prominence. A slow smile of satisfaction slashed Nikolai's forbidding mouth. He was very much looking forward to the evening ahead. It would *kill* Cyrus to see the woman he wanted with his mortal enemy.

And that was what the entire exercise was all about, he reminded himself darkly. Striking a blow at Cyrus was the goal, *not* taking Ella to bed. He tensed. Taking Ella to bed to taste that soft white skin, play with those luscious little breasts and sink so deep into her that she wouldn't know where he began and she ended. The erotic images sizzled through his brain, cutting through rational thought. Hunger thrummed through him instead, kicking off the pulse at his groin until he throbbed with hungry need. His even white teeth gritted while he fought the reaction because this wasn't how it was supposed to be.

On the bottom step, Ella collided with Nikolai's scorching dark golden eyes and her heart started banging like crazy inside her chest, every sense switching to super-sensitive levels. He was so beautiful it hurt. The luxuriant black of his hair, the sculpted slant of his hard cheekbones, the clean-shaven shadow outlining his strong jaw and wonderfully sensual and kissable lips. Taken aback by her own susceptibility, she sucked in a hasty breath and walked out to the waiting limousine with him.

'I understand that this was your grandfather's house. How long is it since he died?' Ella asked quietly.

Nikolai tensed, long tanned fingers curling against a powerful thigh. 'Five years.'

'Were you close?'

'No, I never met him…'

'Never?' Ella studied him wide-eyed. 'And yet he left you his house?'

'And his vast business empire. He wasn't a sentimental man but having an heir of his own blood was tremendously important to him,' Nikolai divulged grudgingly, loathing the topic of conversation but too proud and private to admit his sensitivity to it.

He had long since come to terms with his grandfather's essential indifference to him as a human being. The old man had paid for his education, and thanks to that Nikolai had been able to build on his strengths and advance in life, he thought. Sadly his grandfather had not been equally generous to Nikolai's sister, Sofia, because his sole interest had been in his *male* grandchild.

Nikolai's conscience was still weighted by the knowledge that his only sibling had had to leave school young, work in menial jobs in Athens and scrimp and save for survival. Even more regrettably he had come into his inheritance too late to protect or help the young woman who had been more of a mother to him than a sister. Sofia had died before he could express his gratitude or show his affection, because as a boy and young man he had been thoughtless and selfish, taking his only sibling for granted while making his home in London where he studied and worked for a pittance in those early years.

'How strange,' Ella remarked and, having picked up on his distaste for the subject, she said no more. She settled into the plush interior of the car.

'This evening if you're asked any nosy questions about our relationship just ignore them. We met last year and now we're together. That's all anyone needs to know,' he told her flatly.

What Nikolai had mentioned was as much as she knew herself, which made it impossible for her to betray any secrets. And were there secrets? Oh, yes, she felt in her bones that there were. But prying was forbidden because she was only with Nikolai for her family's benefit, she reminded herself firmly. She wasn't planning to get involved with him or his life or his secrets. Neither was she about to take an interest in his preferences or his moods. As far as possible she would keep herself as detached as he was. In the circumstances that was her first and only line of defence.

'Have you got that?' Nikolai prompted in the silence.

'Right. Got it,' Ella made a teasing zipping motion along her mouth. 'No chatterbox here to worry about.'

Nikolai studied her in surprise. With that dancing

sparkle in her eyes and the cheeky tilt to her chin below the almost smiling, upward curve of her lush lips, she looked radiant. Involuntarily his gaze lingered. 'You're beautiful,' he said without meaning to.

Disconcertion widened her eyes and she flushed, turning her head away to look out at the city streets flashing past the window. In the flare of the street lights his eyes had changed from onyx dark and guarded to that melted caramel shade she was so partial to and butterflies had fluttered in her tummy. Butterflies, as if she were a blasted schoolgirl! she scolded herself in disgust. Was there some foolish part of her trying to romanticise his plans for her? Yes, Nikolai Drakos wanted her…but only for a little while. He didn't want her to keep. He didn't want to get to know her concerns or share them. Sex would be superficial, fleeting. She had to stay sensible or she would get hurt because he was a terrifyingly attractive man, whose mystery simply gave him added depth.

As they left the limousine Nikolai banded a hand to her back. Her spine was rigid. She was as tense as he was. 'By the way, you might see your old friend Cyrus Makris tonight.'

Ella frowned. 'Cyrus isn't back from China yet.'

'He is,' Nikolai contradicted. 'But if he's here tonight you don't speak to him.'

Aghast at the command, Ella twisted round to look at his lean dark features, recognising the hardness etched there. 'But—'

'No argument. You're with me now. You cut him dead,' Nikolai instructed harshly.

'Nikolai, that's not fair.'

'I never promised to play fair,' he murmured impatiently as a stout older woman clad in a sequinned dress hailed him with enthusiasm.

Nikolai seemed to know everyone and a great wave of introductions engulfed Ella. Pre-dinner drinks were being served when a woman moved to a podium to make a speech about the victims of domestic abuse. By the time she had finished speaking, Nikolai had embarked on a conversation with two men and with a whisper Ella headed off to find the cloakroom.

And that was the moment when she finally saw Cyrus. He crossed the foyer to intercept her. He was smaller, slighter than Nikolai, blond and blue-eyed with wings of grey at the temples. 'Ella... I couldn't believe it was you. What on earth are you doing here?'

Ella reddened, uneasy with the intensity of his stare and the angry flush on his cheeks. 'I was planning to ring you but we haven't spoken since you left.'

'Your grandmother told me you were in London but said she didn't have your address.'

'I haven't had the chance to give it to her yet. I only arrived here today,' she told him uncomfortably, forced to come to a halt when he closed a hand round her wrist, his grip painfully tight. 'I've met someone, Cyrus.'

'How is that possible? You hardly go out.'

'You were always telling me to go out,' she reminded him.

'*Not* to find another man!' he disclaimed angrily. 'Who is he?'

'Nikolai Drakos...he's a—'

Cyrus's grip on her went limp and then fell away altogether. He frowned in disbelief. 'You're here in London with Drakos?'

Ella nodded slowly, watching a further flush of colour redden Cyrus's face while his mouth flattened into a livid line. 'We have to talk about this. Drakos is a complete bastard with women! He's notorious. How the hell did this happen?'

'Ella…'

The voice was cold as ice but she already knew it as well as she knew her own. A shiver of cold ran down her spine as she turned her head slowly and saw Nikolai glowering at her from several feet away.

'Cloakroom,' she mumbled and fled.

Cyrus simply walked away as fast as he could. He had never stood up to Nikolai, never allowed the younger man the opportunity to confront him. He was a little weasel, brutal with those physically weaker but a complete coward with other men.

'Well, that was a very special viewing. Cyrus is devastated,' an older woman paused by Nikolai's elbow to remark. 'It's only been a couple of weeks since I sent you that email. You certainly don't let the grass grow under your feet.'

'No, I got the girl,' Nikolai conceded. 'Does that make you happy, Marika?'

'Seeing my brother suffer always makes me happy,' she admitted, her dark eyes even colder than Nikolai's. 'And you're a hero. Pat yourself on the back. You've saved the girl from whatever disgusting plans he had for her. I don't think there's enough money in the world to compensate a woman for what life with Cyrus would entail.'

As Nikolai hovered awaiting Ella's reappearance, he acknowledged that the very last thing he felt just then was heroic. Naked rage had stormed through him when he saw Cyrus touching Ella, fondling her wrist like the dirty old man he was. He had almost forgotten where he was and his innate aggression had almost spilled over into violence. And that reality deeply disturbed him.

Why had he got so worked up? On the rare occasions that he saw Cyrus, he was accustomed to blanking him and Cyrus made it easier still by avoiding him. But somehow seeing Ella that close to Cyrus had outraged and revolted him. Hadn't he warned her not to speak to him? Didn't she ever listen? Had she no sense of self-preservation? Nostrils flaring, Nikolai gritted his teeth on a fierce surge of temper.

He knew he was no hero. A real hero would have *saved* his sister. His abject failure in that department had devastated him. He knew that, accepted that, was aware he had never really felt anything emotional since Sofia's death. Nor did he want to feel anything because feeling love was a weakness and it made you a target.

CHAPTER FIVE

ELLA FRESHENED UP in the cloakroom.

Her hands were shaking and her wrist ached where Cyrus had held it too tight. The instant she had seen his anger Gramma's warning had come back to haunt her. An old friend might have been annoyed by being left out of the loop about her move to London but Cyrus had been enraged, incredulous. In the past he had repeatedly urged her to socialise more but apparently not to find *another* man, he had angrily declared.

Suddenly everything Ella had believed she knew about Cyrus had been thrown into turmoil. Surely she was wrong, surely she had to be wrong?

Troubled, she looked back on the history of their relationship. Before Paul's illness was diagnosed he had applied to Cyrus for a working placement in one of the older man's businesses.

'Yes, I'm trying to pull strings because he's my uncle but why shouldn't I?' Paul had said defensively. 'My mother was the daughter of a very rich Greek but she was thrown out of the family for marrying my father because he was British and poor by their standards. Cyrus is her brother. I'll have to hope that he's not as prejudiced as his father.'

Ella had been with Paul the first time he'd met his uncle and Cyrus had given him the placement. Later he had invited them both to his country house and had pledged his support while Paul was ill. He had not let them down either, Ella recalled unhappily. Yes, Cyrus had been different with her tonight but wasn't there some excuse for his anger? He was a friend but she certainly hadn't treated him like a friend. She could've told him she was coming to London with Nikolai, but she hadn't because Nikolai had insisted that no one other than her family and Rosie was allowed to know that she was leaving home.

Ella glided back to Nikolai's side and within minutes they were being seated at their table. There was no opportunity for any private conversation but Nikolai's grim profile and clipped speech spoke for him. Nikolai was angry with her and what remained of the evening passed in an uncomfortable blur. He had told her to cut Cyrus dead and she had disobeyed. But how could she cut dead the man who had found Paul an apartment close to the hospital where he had been receiving treatment? The man who had housed him and hired a nurse to care for him while he was dying? The man who had been by her side when Paul had breathed his last? Tears burned at the backs of Ella's eyes.

Cyrus had said that Nikolai was a complete bastard with women, *and* notorious. And wasn't his treatment of Ella the living proof of that? Was that immoral choice he had given her to be his get-out clause? Her body in return for her family's security and happiness? But she had agreed and, what was more, had sworn she would not make a big drama over it. So where did that leave her? Up the creek without a paddle, she reckoned wretchedly.

'You're furious with me,' she breathed to break the intolerable silence in the limousine returning them to the apartment.

'We'll discuss it when we get back to the house,' Nikolai breathed darkly, lounging back in his corner of the limo and splaying his lean, powerful thighs as he surveyed her.

She had defied him in spite of his instructions. Mutiny was etched in the set of her delicate jawline, obstinacy in the jut of her determined little chin. And damn her but it made him want her more than ever! How was that possible when she was crossing him at every turn? It was irrational and he was not an irrational man. He could, of course, have told her the truth about Cyrus, but she probably wouldn't believe him because he suspected she had seen a side of Cyrus granted to few. He could not risk telling Ella anything because how could he possibly know that he could trust her?

But his inability to trust wasn't uppermost in his mind at that moment. Acting on impulse, he slid along the passenger seat and gathered her stiff little body into his arms.

'What the—?' Ella gasped, jerking in stark disconcertion.

'He shouldn't have touched you,' Nikolai growled against her parted lips. 'You're not *his* to touch.'

And he crushed her soft, full mouth under his with all the hunger powering him. She went limp and kissed him back, a little whimper escaping her as his tongue flicked against hers. He felt her arms come up round his neck and he almost smiled. Talking was a vastly overrated exercise. Sometimes action talked louder and she was his, indisputably *his* when he touched her, her lithe little body curling into him, one hand stroking his shoulder, the other delving into his hair.

Nikolai thought of lifting the skirt of her gown, swivelling her round, ripping off her panties and sating the overwhelming need that was making him ache. Black lashes lifting, he wrenched his mouth free of the clinging passion of hers and released a long shuddering sigh.

'I'm burning up for you. I spent the day planning what I want to do with you in bed.'

'I spent the day bored out of my mind at that beauty salon,' Ella confided helplessly. 'What did you plan to do?'

Nikolai whispered and her bones melted like honey, desire clenching her feminine core and tightening her nipples into straining buds.

'Not to be recommended even in a limo,' Nikolai concluded as he settled her circumspectly back in her corner of the seat. 'But a guy can dream…'

Ella smoothed down her skirt and fought to catch her breath. His words had undone her. She was with a male who could be bold and unconventional when he felt the urge. The price? Now she was all overheated and quivery and wanton and shocked at herself. Only minutes earlier she had been resentful and confused and unbearably tense but he had contrived to release that tension in the most unexpected way.

Nikolai followed her into the truly hideous drawing room with its swagged and canopied drapes and looming dark furniture. It put him in mind of a funeral parlour and he wished he had had the time to throw in an interior decorator to modernise the place. 'So, tell me,' he urged ruefully. 'What were you playing at tonight with Cyrus?'

'I spoke to Cyrus because he's a friend.'

Nikolai reacted as fast as a whip. He grabbed her hand and turned up her slender wrist where the skin was now showing purpling black fingerprints. 'A *friend* did this?' he growled in disbelief.

'It was an accident. He was angry because I hadn't told him that I was leaving home. I'm sure he didn't mean to hurt me!' Ella protested, snatching her hand back protectively. 'What's it to you anyway?'

'I'm the one responsible for your safety and, let me tell you now, you are *not* safe with Cyrus. Don't ever be alone with him anywhere,' Nikolai bit out forcefully.

'That's a ridiculous thing to say,' Ella framed in bewilderment. 'He warned me off you too.'

Nikolai threw back his head. 'Did he indeed?'

'He said you were a complete bastard with women, *notorious*,' she recited curtly.

'If being honest about my lack of honourable or long-term intentions is being a bastard, then I'm guilty as charged. Do you want a drink?'

'White wine,' she muttered. 'Th—thanks.' Her voice tripped on the word as he pressed a wine glass into her hand.

Nikolai tipped back his brandy in an unappreciative gulp. 'I need you to do as I ask, Ella, not as you want.'

'I need you to be human…seems we're both destined to disappointment,' she whispered round the rim of her glass.

'I don't handle disappointment well. For your own

sake, stay away from Cyrus,' he breathed in a driven undertone.

Ella studied him and wondered how he could expect her to trust him over Cyrus when Cyrus had already earned her trust. Incomprehension assailed her because Nikolai was by no means slow on the uptake. The two men disliked each other; she had got that message loud and clear from both of them. The difference between them was in her reaction. Cyrus's behaviour had confused and troubled her but, inexplicably, Nikolai's reaction tore her up inside. And she didn't know why. She had no more idea why when she looked at his lean, darkly handsome features and sensed vulnerability, because from the outside Nikolai didn't have a vulnerable bone in his big, powerful body.

Max knocked at the door and offered supper. Both of them declined and the pitter-patter of running paws on the tiled hall floor announced the entry of the dogs. Rory hurled herself joyfully against Nikolai's legs while Butch bounced around Ella, stayed just long enough to get a pat and then went to join Rory.

'I was surprised you had a pet,' Ella admitted abstractedly.

Nikolai glanced at her and straightened from greeting the shaggy little mongrel at his feet. 'I can't take the applause for that. Rory belonged to my sister. She called her Princess Aurora…my sister had a love of all things fairy tale,' he murmured stiffly, his lean, strong face shadowing. 'After she died, I couldn't bring myself to part with her dog, so I kept her.'

'I didn't know you'd lost someone,' she muttered as the dogs raced out again in pursuit of Max.

'Most of us have by the time we reach our third decade.'

'Doesn't make coping with it any easier,' Ella remarked.

A phone rang and Nikolai dug a cell out of his pocket and answered it. As soon as he did she saw his face change, paling and clenching hard. 'I'll be there as soon as I can.'

'What is it? What's happened?'

'There's been a fire…at my hotel. I need to get over there.'

'My goodness…is there anything I can do to help?' Ella exclaimed.

'No, just go to bed. I'll see you later…most probably tomorrow.'

After his sudden departure, Ella walked out to the cosy room off the kitchen where Max was watching television with the dogs at his feet. He stood up. 'Did you change your mind about supper?'

'No. I didn't.' Ella told him about the fire. 'I didn't know Nikolai owned a hotel.'

'The Grand Illusion. He worked in the bar there when he was a student,' Max told her. 'It was also his first big business project. He bought it and turned it into one of the most sought-after boutique hotels in Europe. I hope it's not too badly damaged. He's very attached to the place.'

Ella slid into the big white bed upstairs. The sheets were cool and silky against her skin. She was alone, reflecting wryly that she had not expected to be alone in bed tonight. She was too tired to agonise over the long eventful day but her body quickened and heated when she remembered Nikolai's mouth on hers in the limo and what he had whispered. There was nothing wrong with wanting him, she told herself drowsily. He was extraordinarily sexy and her response was simply natural and normal. Why did she feel guilty about what couldn't be helped? After all, no power on earth could bring back Paul or the future life she had once dreamt of sharing with him. Less troubled than she had been earlier, she finally slept.

When she wakened it was almost nine and she was very hungry. She discovered that Max had unpacked her clothes into one of the built-in closets off the passageway that led into the en suite and she picked out jeans and a long-sleeved tee before she went for a shower. Nikolai had not returned during the night. Either he had slept elsewhere or he was still dealing with the aftermath of the fire. While she applied a little make-up, her nose wrinkling at that newly acquired vanity, she was still thinking about that passionate kiss in the limousine and questioning how one kiss could possibly be that special.

As she emerged from the bathroom the bedroom door opened and Nikolai appeared. He looked exhausted and he brought with him the acrid smell of smoke. He stared at her with red-rimmed eyes and for a split second it was as though he didn't know who she was or what she was doing there.

'How was it?' she asked uncertainly.

Momentarily he closed his eyes and a faint shudder racked his lean, strong frame. 'Horrible...' he finally rasped, kicking back his shoulders to shrug off his jacket. 'I stink of smoke. I need a shower.'

'Was anyone hurt?' she pressed.

Halfway through unbuttoning his shirt, he looked at her, dark deep-set eyes semi-closed with no lightening flare of gold. 'Yes. I was at the hospital before I came back. Three of my staff are injured. One has...' his voice roughened '...life-changing injuries.'

'I'm sorry, Nikolai. You knew him personally?' she prompted sickly.

As the shirt fell to the floor he nodded in silence. 'I worked with the kitchen and bar staff as a student. The fire started behind the hotel. There was an explosion. Two assistant chefs were hurt. The bar manager has severe burns and he's facing years of surgery,' he completed gruffly.

'I'm so very sorry,' she said again, because she could see by the fierce tightness of his facial muscles that it had all been almost more than he could bear. He was literally fighting to stay in control and, shamefully, the tears glimmering in his dark eyes fascinated her.

'It could've been worse,' he said as if he was reminding himself of that reality in an effort to stave off too much negativity. 'The guests all got out in time. The hotel's wrecked but bricks and mortar can be rebuilt. It's lives that can't.'

He toed off his shoes, yanked off his socks and peeled off his trousers in his determined path to the shower. She could see that he wasn't even conscious that he was stripping naked in front of her. The lithe bronzed perfection of his lean, powerful body was revealed and she strove to respect his lack of awareness by not staring. He was drained and devastated and in a state she had never expected to see him in.

'Can I get you anything?'

'Max met me on the way in. He's bringing up breakfast...not sure I'll be able to eat,' he mumbled thickly.

Ella became braver. She moved into the bathroom doorway. 'It's not your fault this happened, Nikolai.'

'It's someone's fault!' he ground out rawly. 'The police suspect arson. An accelerant was used. Plastic bins shoved up against the oil tanks caused the explosion. It was no accident.'

'Oh, my word,' she whispered, moving back to the bedroom.

Max brought a covered tray and told her that he had included her in the food order. Butch pranced round her feet with Rory, both of them wanting to stay, but she asked Max to take the dogs back downstairs.

'He's shattered. He needs to rest,' Max agreed. 'Sleep makes everything look less dire.'

Nikolai reappeared, a towel wrapped round his narrow waist, damp black hair flopping untidily over his brow. Ella poured coffee and thrust a knife and fork at him as he sank down in one of the chairs by the table at the window.

'Eat,' she urged. 'You need fuel for energy.'

His wide, sensual mouth quirked as he met anxious green eyes. She was all warmth and softness but her sympathy unnerved him. He had learned to get by without leaning on anyone and it had protected him over and over again from making dangerous mistakes. If he didn't give his trust, it couldn't be broken. If he didn't open up to other people, he couldn't get hurt. Well, OK, he was hurting now, but that couldn't be helped because that was the kind of damage that life threw at everybody. Only this time, someone had personally choreographed that damage, he reminded himself grimly. Who hated him enough to target a packed hotel with an arson attack? Nikolai knew how fortunate it was that so many people had escaped the fire unscathed.

He drank the coffee and ate some bacon but admitted that he had no appetite. Ella wanted to ask him more about the fire but reckoned that a tactful silence was more welcome.

'I'll go to bed. I have to go back to the police station later,' Nikolai told her wearily, walking back to the bathroom.

She heard drawers open and close and when he reappeared he had disposed of the towel and donned a pair of tight-fitting white cotton boxers. For an instant she stared because he was so beautifully built, from his well-defined pectorals to the inverted V of muscle above his hips. She was surprised to see an elaborate tattoo adorning one masculine shoulder. It depicted a winged goddess...and a tiny *unicorn*? What was that all about? Her mouth drying, she swallowed hard and snatched up the book she had abandoned beside the bed the night before.

'I'll see you later,' she said breathlessly as she scooped up the big tray to take it downstairs in the lift.

Fatigue overwhelmed Nikolai. There were things he had wanted to say to Ella but he couldn't remember what they were. Instead he found himself recalling the tenderness, the caring in her shimmering green eyes while she tried to nag him into eating. It had reminded him of the way his sister had looked at him when he was sick as a little boy. With a savage curse he blocked out the disturbing image of both.

*　*　*

Ella settled at the kitchen table while Max baked a cake and talked about his army days. The dogs trotted in and out of the back garden. When the doorbell buzzed, she followed him out to the hall and then hovered, unsure why she had done so. When she saw Cyrus smiling on the doorstep she stiffened in dismay, but then he saw her and smiled warmly at her and she discovered that she couldn't hold spite against the man over bruises that were already fading from her wrist.

'Cyrus…' she said, moving forward.

'I hoped that I'd find you home today,' Cyrus remarked, extending a huge bouquet of flowers, which Ella passed uneasily to Max.

The whole situation felt wrong to her and she was very uncomfortable. Cyrus and Nikolai thoroughly disliked each other and she knew without even being told that Nikolai would be furious that Cyrus had entered his home. Yet Cyrus's calm manner and friendly smile were far more familiar to her than the angry man he had been the night before.

'Come in,' she said, struggling to feel more welcoming.

'I'll make you some tea before I leave to do the shopping,' Max promised.

'I knew you wouldn't be expecting me.' Cyrus followed her into the dark drawing room where he glanced around and rolled his eyes without comment. 'But I couldn't leave things the way they were when we parted last night.'

'It was awkward,' she conceded.

Cyrus took a seat and asked her about her family. She was very careful about what she said, fearful that he would ask difficult questions about her father's failed business because she had promised Nikolai that she would not discuss the matter. In actuality Cyrus made no reference to the debts or of the fact that the shop had closed and she realised that it was perfectly possible that he had no idea of the financial mess her family had been in.

'I have a question to ask you and it may surprise you,' Cyrus warned her as Max brought in a tray.

Taken aback, Ella studied him uncertainly. 'Is it likely to upset me?'

'I hope not.' Cyrus smiled again while she poured the tea. 'I've known you over four years, Ella. Recently, however, it's become a challenge for me to be the friend you want and if I've seen less of you that is why.'

Ella was becoming increasingly tense but she said nothing.

'You're worth much more than some tawdry affair with Drakos. I want to take you away from here *today*,' he told her emphatically. 'I want you to marry me. I'm asking you to be my wife.'

Her tummy gave a queasy lurch at the mere concept of that but she was careful to keep her face composed because, no matter how outlandish and inappropriate she found his proposal, she was still reluctant to hurt him. 'I'm afraid I've never seen you in that light, Cyrus. I think of you as Paul's uncle and a good friend.'

'Clearly I've played the waiting game too long and too well,' Cyrus said drily. 'I didn't want to make our relationship uncomfortable.'

Ella had never felt more uncomfortable with Cyrus than she did at that moment. She didn't like the way he was looking at her. If he had feelings for her, she could not return them and there was no way to wrap that wounding fact up as a compliment. 'I do like and respect you.'

'I should've spoken up sooner. You being here with Drakos suggests that I waited too long to tell you how I feel.' Cyrus could not hide his loathing for Nikolai or his contempt as he voiced his name. 'But I couldn't help being aware that you had an abnormal relationship with my nephew and I didn't want to put pressure on you.'

Ella had fallen very still. 'Abnormal? In what way?'

'Well, it certainly wasn't normal for the two of you to be in a celibate engagement,' Cyrus declared with a caustic derision that sent mortified colour flying into her cheeks. 'You should know that by the time of his death Paul had no secrets from me.'

Severely discomfited, Ella turned from red to bone white and curved her hands tightly round her cup as if savouring that warmth.

'But that wasn't your fault…it was *his*. I was tempted to tell you what I knew after the funeral but I didn't see that telling you that late in the day would be doing you any favours.'

Frowning, Ella leant forward in a sudden movement and put her cup back on the tray with a sharp little snap. 'Telling me what, for goodness' sake?'

'Paul was involved in a homosexual relationship before he met you.'

Ella stared at him in complete disbelief. 'That's a total lie!' she gasped.

'I don't know if he was gay, bisexual or simply confused, but Paul was definitely not attracted to women in the usual way,' Cyrus continued in the same hectoring tone of superiority. 'And once Paul realised he was ill, he clung to you for comfort and support and you gave it unstintingly. That's why he asked you to marry him. He was terrified of losing you and being alone.'

'It's not true,' Ella insisted in shock. 'It *can't* be true.'

'I'm afraid it is true,' Cyrus told her, curtly impatient. 'And that background made it very difficult for me to know how best to proceed.'

Ella stood up in the hope of hastening his departure. 'There was nothing to proceed with,' she muttered in fierce rebuttal. 'Even if it is, I'm not attracted to you as a man.'

Cyrus rose as well and moved closer. 'How would you even *know*, Ella? You've never been with a *real* man.'

Rage finally filtered through Ella's shock and freed her to speak her mind. 'Paul was more of a real man than you'll ever be! A good relationship isn't necessarily dependent on sex.'

'Let me show you what you're rejecting out of misplaced loyalty!' Cyrus grated, reaching for her. 'Did you even listen to me? I did you the honour of asking you to marry me!'

'Don't touch me!' Ella stepped sideways, only to be entrapped by the hand that closed roughly into her hair and yanked. Tears sprang to her eyes because it hurt. 'Let go of me!'

Cyrus had gone all red and his face was a mask of offended fury. 'I have every right to touch you!' he hurled down at her, his other hand biting into her slight shoulder. 'I spent a fortune helping Paul but it was all for *your* benefit. Are you aware that Drakos is the son of a drug dealer and a whore? Doesn't that matter to you?'

With every angry word he was pushing her backwards and her calves hit the base of the sofa and his bullying momentum toppled her down on top of it.

'I'm going to show you what you've been missing,' he intoned viciously.

CHAPTER SIX

Upstairs, Nikolai had stirred when the doorbell had rung and had then flinched when the front door had slammed loudly on Max's exit. When his cell phone began ringing beside the bed, he groaned in frustration and gave up the attempt to continue sleeping.

He checked his watch as he lifted his phone. He had had a couple of hours and that would have to do, he reasoned, springing out of bed and raking his fingers through his tousled black hair. Talking on the phone, he strode into the bathroom to splash his face and froze halfway there as his brain kicked in and he recognised the controlled distress in the voice he was listening to. His shoulders slumped as he voiced his sympathy at yet another piece of bad news and then he tossed his phone down in disgust. The bar manager had passed away shortly after Nikolai had left the hospital.

He had pulled on jeans and was wandering barefoot back into the bedroom when a flash of bright colour outside attracted his attention. The drapes hadn't been pulled properly. A very distinctive car was parked on the other side of the road. It was a bright yellow Ferrari and Nikolai knew exactly who that car belonged to. For a split second he couldn't credit the coincidence and then it dawned on him that Ella was in the house and he couldn't relax until he had checked on her. He raced downstairs, saw the drawing-room door ajar, heard Ella's muffled shriek of pain and kicked the door wide.

Suddenly the weight pinning Ella to the sofa was gone. She blinked in bewilderment and shock as Cyrus went flying back against the wall opposite where Nikolai had flung him after dragging him off her. She sat up just as Nikolai punched the older man hard in the stomach and shouted at him in Greek. Cyrus had attacked her, had torn at her jeans and she was bruised and sore and shaken and frightened. Only the fear that Nikolai might kill Cyrus made her intervene. She stumbled across the room and wrenched at Nikolai's arm.

'No…no, don't hit him again. You've hurt him enough!' she gasped as Cyrus, blood running down his face, which was already swelling from several hits, dragged himself up clumsily from the floor and stumbled frantically towards the door.

'He *hurt* you!' Nikolai vented between gritted white teeth as he strode after the fleeing older man.

Again, Ella grabbed his arm to hold him back and give Cyrus enough time to make it out through the front door. 'If you kill him you'll go to prison for it… is that what you want?'

A string of Greek curses erupted from Nikolai as Ella slammed the door protectively in his enemy's wake. 'I should've warned you about him.'

'You told me not to be alone with him. I didn't pay any heed,' she mumbled guiltily.

'He's been accused of getting rough with women before,' Nikolai divulged.

Blood dripped down onto the polished wooden floor

and she grabbed his hand to examine his bruised and bleeding knuckles. 'You need cleaning up,' she said, angling him towards the stairs.

'What happened before he attacked you?'

'He asked me to marry him and when I told him I wasn't interested he went off in a rage,' she told him in a daze. 'If Gramma hadn't already hinted to me that she thought he had a more than personal interest in me, I would've been gobsmacked. As it was, I tried to be polite. It never once occurred to me that he could be thinking of me like that.'

So, Cyrus had proposed. He *had* intended marriage. It should've been a moment of triumph for Nikolai but it fell resoundingly flat. He had wounded his opponent but Ella had been wounded too. He was appalled that Cyrus had contrived to violently assault Ella and he felt incredibly guilty about that reality. After all, he knew exactly what Cyrus was like and he had virtually set Ella up as a target for the older man's frustrated rage. She could've been raped just as his sister had been and the mere concept of Ella enduring such a violation made Nikolai feel sick with guilt and self-loathing. He was supposed to be in control of events, but somewhere along the line of his plotting he had become selfish and reckless and Ella had very nearly paid the ultimate price. How irresponsible was that?

Even worse, Ella was now valiantly trying to urge him up the stairs as if he were the injured party and in need of the support of her tiny frame. In another mood he would have laughed at the incongruity of her sympathy for him at that moment. But he was not in a laughing mood any more than he was in a triumphant one.

'What did he do to you?' Nikolai demanded, thrusting open the bedroom door.

'He was trying to kiss me and I twisted my face away and he yanked at my hair. I swear he pulled a handful of it out by the roots,' she whispered, massaging her sore scalp. 'He flattened me on the sofa and started pulling at my clothes. I never thought of him as a big, strong man but he was much stronger than me. I don't think I could've got him off me without your help... Thank you.'

'No, don't thank me,' Nikolai said with distaste. 'This is all my fault.'

'I don't see how,' Ella pronounced, dabbing the blood from his hand and applying an antiseptic she had found in the cabinet. She was still trembling in shock from Cyrus's assault and wondering in disbelief what had come over the older man. Had he simply lost his head in temper? Would he really have raped her? Fear and revulsion curdled low in her stomach. He had tried to rip off her jeans, she recalled with a shudder. There could be no mistake about the motivation of his attack.

'His conduct is nothing to do with you,' Ella continued a little unevenly as her breathing began to settle back to normal levels. 'I was the one who kept up the friendship with Cyrus after Paul died. I used to talk about Paul with his uncle. I needed that outlet after the funeral.'

She fell silent, finally allowing herself to consider what Cyrus had told her about Paul. All the insecurities she had ever felt in her fiancé's radius briefly returned to haunt her. Paul had been a real extrovert and very popular and when she had first known him she had very quickly fallen for him and longed for more than friendship. But nothing had come of her hopes until Paul had fallen ill. That was when she had become important to Paul and when he had first told her that he loved her. Her eyes prickling and burning, she crushed the memory, which now seemed soiled.

There was no point in revisiting the past and allowing Cyrus's allegations to upset her. Paul was gone and her questions couldn't be answered now. But was it possible that she had been blind to the reality of a man's sexual lack of interest? Had she wasted four years of her life on a non-relationship? That was a very distressing thought.

'We should've called the police on Cyrus,' Nikolai breathed in a savage undertone. 'Had him arrested for what he did to you—'

'But thanks to you he didn't really *do* anything. He certainly scared me out of my wits for a few minutes but I wouldn't want to involve the police. He was incredibly generous to Paul while he was ill and, even though today he insisted that he only did all that for *my* benefit, I have to stay grateful for what he did do to help then,' she framed shakily.

'You're crying...' Nikolai registered belatedly as a solitary tear dropped on his hand.

Ella crammed a hand defensively against her wobbling mouth. 'Sorry—'

'No, let it out...you've had a very frightening experience,' Nikolai pointed out, furious that he had let her stand there ministering to his minor injuries when she herself had been through so much more. Without hesitation he bent and swept her up into his arms. 'You need to lie down for a while.'

'Do you really think he would have r-ripped off my clothes *and*…?'

'Yes, I do think that,' Nikolai admitted as he rested her down gently on the disordered bed and sat down beside her. 'Obviously he had wanted you for a very long time and your rejection would have hurt his ego. Make no mistake; Cyrus thinks he's a hell of a good catch.'

'To accept that all this time he's been thinking of me like that and I hadn't a clue…it's *horrible*!' Ella broke off with a sudden sob and Nikolai lifted her up into his arms, muttering what sounded like soothing things in Greek.

Ella let the tears fall against his shoulder, belatedly appreciating that he wasn't wearing a shirt, that indeed all he was wearing was his jeans. He felt so hot against her cheek, like a muscular furnace, but she felt so incredibly safe and protected in his arms. 'I'm sorry… so sorry about this.'

'What are you sorry for? Cyrus assaulted you.'

'He said that Paul had had a gay affair,' she confided jaggedly, her heart beating like a hammer inside her. 'And the awful thing is that it might be true and I'll never really know *why* Paul—'

Comprehension entered Nikolai and he breathed in slow and deep. 'It doesn't matter now.'

But it mattered to Ella, who had on several occasions felt humiliated by Paul's physical restraint with her. Even Gramma had been surprised when Paul hadn't asked Ella to move in with him. Had Paul *ever* wanted that kind of intimacy with her? His resistance had made her feel like less of a woman. The suspicion that that might have all been a front to hide his secret cut even deeper because she had believed that they were as close as two people could be without sex.

'Cyrus would have said anything to sully your memories of his nephew,' Nikolai opined. 'He must've been very jealous of him.'

'No, the worst thing is that I'm scared that Cyrus was telling the truth about Paul…a truth I was too stupid to see on my own!' Ella gasped against a smooth, tanned shoulder, marvelling that she could be that close with Nikolai without him making any kind of move on her even though she knew how much he wanted her. That, she conceded dizzily, was yet one more striking difference between Cyrus and Nikolai. Nikolai wasn't taking advantage, *wouldn't* take advantage of her while she was upset. A vague sense of frustration and regret trickled through her in response to that recognition.

Nikolai usually ran a mile from crying women and he was at a loss with Ella. He didn't hug but that was all right because she was the one doing the hugging. He didn't know what to say, though, particularly when she referred to a gay affair. He was definitely out of his element there. Changing the subject struck him as the only possible option and he breathed in deep. 'Desmond, the bar manager in the burns unit, died an hour after I left the hospital,' he told her. 'His son phoned to tell me.'

Ella froze and then jerked up her head to look at him. Her face was flushed and her little nose was red but her green eyes were wet and impossibly appealing, Nikolai registered helplessly. 'I'm so sorry, Nikolai.'

'He was a good guy,' Nikolai volunteered. 'I met him when I started working at the hotel. I was only eighteen. He trained me…'

FREE Merchandise is 'in the Cards' for you!

Dear Reader,

We're giving away FREE MERCHANDISE!

Seriously, we'd like to reward you for reading this novel by giving you **FREE MERCHANDISE** worth over $20 retail. And no purchase is necessary!

You see the Jack of Hearts sticker above? Paste that sticker in the box on the Free Merchandise Voucher inside. Return the Voucher promptly...and we'll send you valuable Free Merchandise!

Thanks again for reading one of our novels—and enjoy your Free Merchandise with our compliments!

Pam Powers

Pam Powers

P.S. Look inside to see what Free Merchandise is **"in the cards"** for you!

W

e'd like to send you two free books like the one you are enjoying now. Your two books have a combined price of over $10 retail, but they are yours to keep absolutely FREE! We'll even send you 2 wonderful surprise gifts. You can't lose!

Detach card and mail today. No stamp needed. ►

© 2015 HARLEQUIN ENTERPRISES LIMITED. ® and ™ are trademarks owned and used by the trademark owner and/or its licensee. Printed in the U.S.A.

FREE MERCHANDISE VOUCHER

> 2 FREE
> BOOKS
> and
> 2 FREE
> GIFTS

Please send my Free Merchandise, consisting of
2 Free Books and **2 Free Mystery Gifts**.
I understand that I am under no obligation to buy
anything, as explained on the back of this card.

❏ I prefer the regular-print edition
   106/306 HDL GKA7

❏ I prefer the larger-print edition
   176/376 HDL GKA7

Please Print

FIRST NAME

LAST NAME

ADDRESS

APT.#   CITY

STATE/PROV.   ZIP/POSTAL CODE

NO PURCHASE NECESSARY!

P-516-FMH16

'What were you like at eighteen?' she whispered, relieved to be sprung from her introspection.

It was yet another one of those occasions when Nikolai found a woman hard to comprehend. What did what *he* was like at eighteen have to do with anything? How was that relevant?

'Cocky…horny,' he murmured blankly, his mind elsewhere as he breathed in the scent of her hair. She smelt like strawberries. Was that her shampoo? He stroked long fingers down the back of her head, watching the bronze strands shimmer like silk in the light. He was hard as a rock below the jeans and that seriously bothered him because it was inappropriate after what Cyrus had done.

Ella tilted her head back and looked up into Nikolai's lean dark face. She saw the raw hunger tightening his spectacular bone structure and the burn in his melted caramel eyes below the black velvet fringe of his lashes. 'You have beautiful eyes,' she told him truthfully, every fibre of her body suddenly prickling with physical awareness.

She had travelled from gay affairs to what he was like as a teenager to his eyes and that only reminded Nikolai why he rarely had conversations with women. He had sex with them and kept the talking to the absolute minimum. His strong jawline clenched. 'I was telling you that Desmond had died…'

Ella felt the heat of shame suffuse her mortified face. 'Yes.'

'His family were with him at the end. He would've wanted that. He was very much a family man,' he breathed gruffly.

And that catch in his dark deep drawl and the anguish he was struggling to contain in his stunning eyes simply fuelled Ella's fascination with the male holding her. Nikolai Drakos was incredibly emotional. That great well of intense emotion was what he hid behind the cold front and he usually hid it well but just at that moment pretence was beyond him and she loved that too. He was being so open with her, so frank and natural. His attitude washed away the bad feelings Cyrus and his revelations had infused her with and she felt her own strength again.

'Not that I know much about how normal families operate,' Nikolai acknowledged thickly.

Her fingers slid over a bare tanned shoulder. His skin felt like satin and the physical heat he put out attracted her as potently as the sun on a cold day. She quivered, awesomely aware of the swelling fullness of her breasts and the prickling tightening of her nipples. She was in control, in full control of herself, yet when she looked at Nikolai it was hard to breathe or swallow because she was remembering what his mouth felt like on hers. And unlike Paul, Nikolai *wanted* her, she reminded herself with satisfaction. Beneath her thigh she could feel him primed and ready, something she had never felt with Paul. Paul hadn't wanted her the way she'd wanted him but Nikolai did and couldn't hide it. That knowledge clenched something deep down inside her and made her feel oddly giddy.

Her hand came up of its own volition and skated along the tempting fullness of his sensual lower lip. His eyes lit up like firecrackers when she met them boldly, wanting, craving, needing and for the very first time unashamed of her natural instincts.

'Was that an invitation?' Nikolai husked, a faint

shudder racking his big, powerful frame because every atom of pent-up energy imprisoned inside him longed for release.

'You need it gilt-edged and engraved?' Ella teased, alight with her own daring, her own decision. He wanted her, she wanted him and it was normal and natural, she told herself firmly, even though somewhere deep down inside herself she was secretly shocked that *she* was the one taking the initiative.

'Oh, no… I'm a much quicker study,' Nikolai told her, sliding her down against the pillows and leaning down to trace her lush smiling mouth with his. In truth he wanted to flatten her to the bed and claim her body and soul like a Neanderthal. It took immense control to remember that she was innocent and deserving of the very best he could deliver.

The aggressive stroke of his tongue between her lips extracted a whimper of sound from the back of Ella's throat. Her whole body pulsed with expectation. She wondered dimly when it had happened, when she had travelled from simply wanting him to the edge of an unbearable craving that she could no longer fight. And she didn't care because there was no later or tomorrow or any kind of future in her thoughts, there was only this one special moment when she was finally making her choice and stepping out beyond the grief that had weighed her down for so long. His mouth crashed down on hers and she welcomed it, tipping her head back, parting her lips, all woman, all welcome. His passion enthralled her as much as the emotion he concealed as though it was something to be ashamed of.

'I swear I could devour you,' Nikolai swore against her swollen mouth.

He gazed down as her dreamy green eyes darkened to emerald, her bronze hair fanning round her head in a halo of vibrant colour. Cyrus had hurt and frightened her yet she still wanted Nikolai. It was a strangely humbling acknowledgement because he knew it meant that she trusted him. And yet he knew that he wasn't worthy of her trust because he hadn't told her what he had done. He crushed that train of thought to attend to the fact that she was still wearing far too many clothes.

Ella watched Nikolai yank off her jeans from the ankles and colour ran up over her chest as her serviceable black knickers were revealed. Nikolai tossed the jeans down and peeled her top off over her head, tumbling tresses falling back on her white shoulders above sweet little breasts cradled in lace cups. He could see her uncertainty, the nervous tension building as if she had no idea that *his* hands were shaking and that he was burning up for her, no idea at all that she was a rare and perfect beauty. He couldn't take his eyes from her as he unclipped the bra and lifted his hands to explore the delicate little mounds he had bared.

'Gorgeous...' he said gruffly, the word torn from him because she looked as though one wrong word from him would send her into flight.

'Seriously?' she pressed, face hot with a heady combination of surprise, embarrassment and doubt.

'Serious as a heart attack.' A long tanned finger stroked a dainty swell crowned by a straining pink nipple and he bent his head to capture it with his mouth. 'I like your breasts. I could even go as far as saying that I *love* your breasts,' he framed, his warm breath fanning her skin as he blew on a straining pink bud.

'But there's nothing much there,' she mumbled almost argumentatively because she had always felt that her lack of endowment in the bosom department was her biggest physical flaw. She was tiny and she was skinny and she didn't have the curves so many men were said to prefer.

'More than enough to satisfy me,' Nikolai growled, long fingers curving to a ripe little mound, gently stroking the responsive flesh, smiling as her back arched, driving her breast into his palm. 'You're delicious.'

Some of her tension ebbed. He wanted her, she reminded herself with growing assurance, and being wanted like that, complimented like that, suddenly seemed like the most wonderful thing in the world. He was accepting her, flaws and all, and in the same way she would accept him, she promised herself. She wasn't going in expecting perfection and eternal love.

The brush of his fingers against a prominent nipple made her hiss and her hips performed a little shimmy all on their own. Her body was warming up at its own pace, warmth gathering in her pelvis, tingles of reaction ensuring that she was fiercely aware of that part of her. He yanked off her knickers with scant ceremony, taking her by surprise. Her eyes flew wide, startled, apprehensive.

Nikolai smiled down at her. 'It's all right. We won't do anything you don't want to do…'

'I want to do everything,' she admitted shakily as he freed her from his weight and slid off the bed. 'Where are you going?'

'Condoms,' he explained, striding into the bathroom. 'There may not be any because I've never used the house…no, there's nothing here.'

'You don't need to,' Ella muttered, shaking her head. 'I have a contraceptive implant in my arm.'

He frowned. 'But why do you have that?'

'When Paul and I were together, I thought…well, that I'd need contraception.' Ella struggled to think back to that period when everything had been shiny and new and untested between her and Paul. As far as she recalled the implant would keep her safe from pregnancy for four years, but try as she did she could not remember exactly when she had had the implant put in.

'I've never had sex without a condom and I've been tested… I'm clean,' Nikolai assured her.

Ella was already thinking about something else. 'A moment ago you said you'd never used this house. *Never?*'

'Never,' he repeated. 'It didn't feel like mine. The day I got the keys I walked over every inch of it and thought what a waste it was that I was never allowed to meet the old guy. There are all these ancient photos of people and I don't know who they are and I never will know now because there's nobody left to identify them. Yet some of them must be relatives.'

'That's sad,' she agreed.

He didn't know why he was talking to her like that because he had been on his own a long time and he liked it that way…didn't he? Once his sister was gone, he had not had a single living relative that he knew of. Of course, he hadn't looked, he acknowledged for the first time, and he was well aware that his grandfather had had sisters because they had contacted him. He had simply decided that it would be pointless at this stage in his life to take the connection any further. And why the hell was he even thinking about such a thing?

What did Ella do to his wits? Why was he confiding in her when she lay naked and beautiful on a bed in front of him? What kind of black magic was that? He was talking about private things that he never ever shared. *Thee mou*, it had to be those soft, sympathetic eyes of hers working a dangerous spell.

'I've never needed family,' he told her flatly.

Ella was wondering if it would be pathetic to slide below the duvet to hide her naked body and she was stiff as a post while she lay there wondering, colour creeping up across her nudity in a mottled flush of awful self-consciousness. It was daylight and the drapes weren't fully closed and everything was on display and she felt incredibly uncomfortable.

'Family's everything to me,' Ella admitted, finally giving up the fight and diving below the duvet with apology. 'I can't imagine life without them.'

'The duvet won't hide you from me for long,' Nikolai warned, the command gilt-edged with the desire clearly burning in his eyes.

He unzipped and dropped his jeans and her eyes rounded at the sight of him because in his haste to check on her earlier he had forgone underwear below the denim. With a sudden laugh, Nikolai pounced and flipped the duvet back off her. 'Was that look one of awe or horror?' he demanded.

Ella's faced burned red. 'No comment...'

Nikolai kissed her breathless and then nipped a line down the slope of her neck that seemed to hit every pulse point she possessed. She gasped beneath his mouth, gasped again when his wickedly clever fingers found her clitoris and lingered with devastating intent. Startled, she jerked, she moaned, lashes fluttering in dazed dismay as he slid down the bed to part her thighs and pay attention to a part of her she much preferred to ignore.

'No, Nik—'

'Is that an embarrassed no? Or an absolutely not?' Nikolai prompted.

Forbearance became the better part of valour and she closed her eyes, trying not to think about what he was planning to do but reluctant to prevent him when her only excuse was shyness. She wasn't that shy, was she? And then he did something that sent a current of red-hot tingles racing through her entire body and her hips executed a sensual shimmy and her lips parted on a long, low whimper and whether she was shy or not got lost in the process. The prickling awareness in her pelvis coalesced into a heavy throb at the heart of her that made her all hot and needy. Suddenly she couldn't worry any more about how she looked or what came next, suddenly she was just in the moment and the moment was so wildly, insanely exciting and primal that she was lost in it. The pulsing heat expanded, sucking in more and more of her and then rising until she couldn't hold it in any more. She gave a helpless cry, her spine arched and her body flailed as an explosive climax gripped her.

'You see, the absolutely not would have been a mistake, *glikia mou*,' Nikolai pointed out as he drew level with her again, eyes like dark melting chocolate caressing her flushed face.

Dumbly she nodded, heart leaping as he claimed her mouth and his tongue tangled with hers in a frank expression of all-male hunger that made her blood thunder through her veins. He was rearranging her limbs, tipping her back into a new position and, before she could even gather all her nerves again, he was there at her entrance and pushing in. At first it felt so strange to her, his body joining with hers, and the sensation of pressure, of stretching, was surprisingly pleasurable, as if her body had been lying in wait for years to experience that exact sensation and was now pouncing on it with joyful acceptance.

And then Ella jerked as a stinging burn marked his invasion. It didn't kill the pleasure but it did make her tense and draw in her breath in dismay.

'Want me to stop?' Nikolai husked, eyes pure, gleaming caramel seduction.

'No...don't you dare!' Ella warned, impatient on the brink of what she had waited so long to experience.

He eased out of her and drove in again and the burn intensified and then vanished. She blinked, expecting pain because she had always expected pain, but the pain didn't arrive. 'It's OK now,' she whispered in surprise.

'It's got to be better than OK for you the first time,' Nikolai told her.

'No expectations here,' she told him bravely and wrapped her arms round him because she recognised his patience, his care and concern and knew it could have been a much less pleasurable experience with someone else.

Her body sang with his every movement, madly stimulated by excitement. Within the space of a minute and a half she travelled from the aftershocks of satiated pleasure to heart-stopping, racing excitement. She angled up to receive him, hips rocking, body thrumming joyfully to the age-old beat of passion. It was good, it was better than good, it was truly amazing to slot helplessly into that fierce hypnotic climb to pleasure again. A kind of frenzy gripped her muscles and she shook, feeling ecstasy within her grasp and snatching at it. And it ran over and through her, a rolling white-hot wave of convulsive delight and fulfilment that left her drained and limp.

Ella was convinced that she would never move again, and then Nikolai moved when she didn't want him to and she rolled over and rested her head on his chest instead, her arm wrapping round his narrow waist.

He dropped a kiss on her damp brow. 'Thank you,' he rasped breathlessly. 'That was amazing.'

She wanted to thank him but she was tongue-tied, everything she had thought she knew about herself, everything she had ever believed, thrown into turmoil. And, quite literally, she couldn't think straight and he felt like the only stable being in an unstable world. A deep sense of peace washed over her in waves of emotional and physical exhaustion.

Nikolai lay still and ever so slightly stiff. Ella was snuggling up to him. He had never snuggled before, was usually straight into the shower, clothes back on, goodbyes said within minutes. Well, isn't this a new experience to be savoured? a sardonic voice sniped inside his head. She deserves *more*, that same little voice added. What sort of more? Nikolai lay there until the even sound of her breathing let him know that she had fallen asleep. Only then did he gently and carefully slide out of the bed.

More as in flowers? He almost smacked his head against the shower wall in frustration. He had never done flowers before. But then he had never had sex with a virgin before. He had never coerced a woman into his bed either while pretending that he was giving her a choice. That final blunt acknowledgement sliced through him as painfully as a knife in the gut. Nausea rising, he got out of the shower and dressed. He would call by his apartment to change into a suit on his way to see Desmond's family and the police. And then what?

Nikolai looked at Ella sleeping in the bed, bronze hair in a mad tangle, a narrow white shoulder and a loosely unfurled tiny hand lying on top of the bedding. She looked so small, so defenceless and he had taken advantage of her. His heart sank. And then what? The question tolled in his conscience like a giant bell and he felt sick again. He had to deal, had no choice really: he had gone too far to turn back.

He sent her a text to explain where he was, which was a serious break from his usual habits. Never apologise, never explain was his usual mantra with women. He sent flowers for the first time in his life. He was almost desperate enough to throw in a cuddly toy as well. By the time he had commiserated with the dead bar manager's family and spent several hours in the police station telling them that, no, he had no idea why anyone would risk the life of so many people by setting his hotel on fire, he was shattered. Of course, he had had to pass on the names of anyone he might deem to have a grudge against him and he had had to mention Cyrus's name in that context. He had been frank with the police, but he had also had to admit that he had not uncovered any actual physical evidence of Cyrus breaking the law and that arson didn't quite run true to form for the man whose sole focus had always been innocent women.

Nikolai returned to his apartment. It was silent and he stood in the low-lit lounge and marvelled at the undeniable truth that in his desire for revenge he had veered badly off course and injured innocents. How had that happened? What had happened to his sense of right and wrong? When had his once pure motivation become twisted? He poured himself a whiskey and sat down in his shirtsleeves, struggling to work out how Ella could ever have struck him as a pawn and as mere collateral damage to be written off.

How could he ever have been that arrogant? That selfish? That wrong? And failed to recognise it? At some stage he had developed a dangerous form of tunnel vision and, seeing only Cyrus in his sights, he had taken aim and fired. Ella was the fallout and, even worse, he might as well have painted a target on her back because Cyrus's violent rage at the town house had been deliberately provoked by Nikolai. He had set her up for that scene and she had been hurt and he was painfully aware that she could have been hurt a lot more.

But how much more would the whole ugly truth hurt Ella? Ella, who was soft enough to sacrifice everything for her family? Ella, who had been unjustly damaged by his pursuit of revenge? He couldn't tell her the truth because that would humiliate and hurt her, inflicting more harm. Another glass of whiskey went down Nikolai's throat as he ran uneasily through all the wounding, shocking blows that Ella had already suffered. The father who had had a stroke, the fiancé who had died, the veterinary career that had had to be put on ice. She had kept on picking herself up and bravely soldiering on and then Nikolai had come along and suddenly everything had taken a turn very much for the worse. He had taken her from her home and her family and her life and then he had taken her to bed. Wrong heaped on wrong heaped on wrong. He raked a trembling hand through his black hair.

How could he possibly tell her that he had set her up and used her as a weapon? What woman's self-esteem could overcome a truth like that? Particularly one who had already had a fiancé who might or might not have had a gay affair?

He owed her.

Somehow, he had to make it up to her. He would give her what he should have given her from the start. Trust, support, stability, respect. Could he fake love? He knew she'd want it, he just didn't know if he could deliver what he'd never felt. He could try though, couldn't he? How hard could it be to say, 'I love you'?

His mobile phone pinged and he looked in consternation at the text she had sent. A black brow slowly lifted in wonderment. She was asking if he was still at the police station and there was a nosy bunny rabbit emoji attached to it.

Thee mou, he was planning to marry a woman who used emoticons…

CHAPTER SEVEN

ELLA WAKENED WITH the sense that something was not quite right in her world. Her hand slid across the empty space beside her and she suppressed a groan because Nikolai had not returned as she had hoped.

One swallow did not a summer make, one of Gramma's favourite sayings. She was not in a relationship with rules where she could develop expectations and act accordingly. No, there were no rules and she felt frighteningly lost without them.

Yet Nikolai had been so different with her the day before. Shorn of his icy, controlled detachment he was a different man. Yesterday he had simmered with passion and emotion. She loved that he had that depth, that capacity for feeling, even though he assiduously hid it from the world. He had been protective, tender and a wonderful lover. In every respect he had been everything she could have wanted, so why was she fretting?

Nobody got to know what tomorrow would bring. She wasn't alone in that situation. Possibly it was Cyrus's revelations about Paul that had left her feeling so unsure of everything. She needed to put what Cyrus had told her away and tuck it back in the past where it belonged. She had genuinely loved and grieved for Paul and nothing could change that. Deep ties of friendship and caring had bound them. And that was the best way to remember him and what they had shared. How he lived before they met was irrelevant and it would be foolish to doubt her own judgment over past events.

As a knock sounded on the door she pushed herself up against the pillows, smiling when Max came in with the dogs trailing in his wake. 'I've set your breakfast out on the deck. It's through the conservatory on the other side of the corridor,' he told her, vanishing into the annexe off the bathroom and emerging with a flowing aqua dressing gown almost too fancy for the description and a pair of slippers.

'Those aren't mine,' she said blankly.

'The closets on the left-hand side in the annexe are packed with your new clothes,' Max explained, snipping off the labels still attached to the garment and settling it down at the foot of the bed for her use.

As Max departed Ella got up and went into the bathroom. She brushed her teeth and ran a brush through her tangled hair before peering into the units she had assumed Nikolai used. A line of female clothing hung there above racks of shoes and the drawers below were filled with separates and fancy lingerie. She sighed and padded back into the bedroom to pull on the robe and slide her feet into the sleek mules.

Rory and Butch awaited her and accompanied her into the conservatory, which had been restored but which was still sadly empty of plants. She walked out onto the deck, which was drenched in sunlight and overlooked the very private garden below. Max had set a tray on the table and she poured herself tea and buttered a piece of toast. She wasn't accustomed to leisure or luxury and what was for her the equivalent of breakfast in bed felt ridiculously decadent and frivolous. The dogs got bored and negotiated the steep spiral staircase that led down to the garden.

Ella sipped her tea and thought about Nikolai. He had probably stayed at his apartment the night before while she had stayed up late wondering when he would return. That had been a mistake and no doubt not the last she would make if she went on trying to squeeze their relationship into a normal frame with potential and boundaries. Sadly it could never be normal; it was a purely temporary arrangement, wasn't it? Nikolai buying her clothes and jewellery would never feel right in such circumstances but she could handle it, couldn't she?

Her family were safe and content and that was what really mattered, she told herself firmly. In three months' time when she was done with Nikolai, she would still have a whole life stretching ahead of her. She shifted in her wrought-iron garden seat, wincing at the soreness at the heart of her, the reminder that she was not quite the same woman she had been yesterday.

Nikolai was amazing in bed. And that was it. It had been good for her because he had *known* how to make it good. It was sex, only sex, just as her relationship with Paul had been more or less only friendship, she acknowledged uncomfortably. Maybe she was destined to have odd one-sided relationships with men, but she was determined that she would protect herself from being hurt again. She was learning from Nikolai, possibly even growing up a little, she reflected ruefully. A year ago she had hated Nikolai for making her want him when she had felt she should still be mourning

Paul, but how could anyone impose a time frame on either the pain and duration of loss or the heat of desire? From the very first Nikolai had lit her up like a firestorm. Her response had been immediate, basic, and utterly instinctive. Trying to prevent it, trying to stamp out the fire, would have been like trying to turn the tide back from the shore.

And Nikolai hadn't tried to turn the tide back either, she ruminated with an abstracted little smile. No, Nikolai had come back for her and had fought to get her into his life and his bed. It gave her the most disturbing guilty kick to be so desired by Nikolai, because with Paul she had always been the one left wanting and feeling inadequate.

Steps rang on the conservatory tiles and she lifted her head.

'Ella...' Nikolai murmured, striding out into the sunlight.

Garbed in a charcoal-grey suit that was exquisitely tailored to his lean, powerful frame, Nikolai took her breath away. He was no longer clean-shaven and the dark stubble demarcating his strong jaw and wide mobile mouth merely added a rougher, more potent edge to his aggressive masculinity. Brilliant dark golden eyes fringed by ebony lashes inspected her.

Mouth running dry, Ella sucked in a sudden breath. He could plunge her into a sea of drowning sexual awareness simply with a look. Her nipples tightened, her body clenched, her slender thighs pressing together tightly. As always he looked spectacular but she did notice that a slightly haggard quality had dulled his usual healthy glow of vigour.

Nikolai stared down at Ella, enchanted by the picture she made. The floaty thing she was wearing was sea green and it pooled around her like a mermaid's tail. In the bright light her perfect skin glowed against her rich bronze hair. Feeling a little less like a man caged and about to hand over the key to his freedom, he dropped down into a seat. *Thee mou*, she was exquisite.

Max arrived with coffee and biscuits. Max, Nikolai ruminated, knowing that that was a problem still to be dealt with: Max had ushered Cyrus into Nikolai's house. The dogs came up the stairs to investigate. At least Butch tried but he was unable to climb the stairs with his three legs and in the end, when he sat whining pitifully on the bottom step, Nikolai took pity on the little animal and went down to lift him and carry him up.

'He'll learn. He's taught himself to go downstairs safely,' Ella commented, but even so she was hugely impressed by his kindness.

'We all learn from our mistakes.' Nikolai lounged back in his chair and rested an ankle across one knee, the fabric of his well-cut trousers pulling taut to delineate the powerful muscles in his thighs. 'For instance, I made a mistake specifying three months with you...'

'Oh...' Ella stilled, her facial muscles locking as if she was in shock. 'Did you?'

'Three months is nothing. I don't want a time limit. I want to keep you,' he advanced levelly, speaking as though what he was saying were not at all personal but simply a matter of business to be taken out and discussed.

'I'm not Butch. I don't think you can just *keep* me,' Ella countered in a slightly wobbly voice, caused by the shock of thinking he wanted to end their arrangement early and then being shot fast in the other direction, only to fail to understand what he was talking about.

'I hope I can if I ask you to marry me,' Nikolai breathed very quietly, assessing dark eyes fringed with black lashes trained to her intently.

'Marry me?' Ella parroted as she straightened up, her shoulders stiffening. 'I asked you to marry me first and *you* said that marriage was out of the question.'

'You were right… I was wrong. Do we have to make a production out of it?' Nikolai asked in the most suspiciously reasonable tone.

Ella was knocked right off balance. In her experience all men found it a challenge to admit to being in the wrong but the admission had just tripped effortlessly off Nikolai's tongue. 'You're asking me to marry you…*now*?'

'Yes. I think we fit together well,' Nikolai declared.

Her wide green eyes couldn't have got any wider. 'In what way?' And her voice lowered. 'In bed?'

'No, I wasn't even thinking about that,' Nikolai lied.

In fascination Ella watched the faintest hint of colour line his sculpted cheekbones and she was tickled pink by the discovery that he could blush. From his point of view the sex genuinely must have been as amazing as he said it was, was all she could initially think. Why else would he be talking about marriage when he had previously been so against the idea?

'So, you want to marry me and keep me,' Ella recounted, thinking that a marriage proposal could not get much more basic and medieval in tone than that.

'Your family will be pleased… I think.'

'Yes, you're right,' Ella conceded, knowing that a wedding ring would make all the difference to her family's concerns because it was a promise of commitment that they trusted.

Nikolai leant forward and closed a hand round hers. 'I intend to do everything within my power to make you happy.'

'That's quite an aspiration.'

'I like to aim high.'

'But I haven't agreed yet.' Ella stared down nervously at the lean tanned hand that had engulfed hers. She glanced up involuntarily and fell into his melted-caramel eyes. Those eyes were as dangerous as a weed-infested pond to a lone swimmer, she thought crazily. She looked into his eyes and butterflies went crazy in her tummy and reasoned thought became too much of a challenge. She was falling for him, she recognised in dismay, falling fast and falling hard for a deeply unscrupulous male, who broke rules and ignored all her boundaries.

'But I'm hoping you will…' His black lashes swept down on his expressive eyes.

Nikolai didn't do fake humility very well, Ella thought in sudden amusement. She wasn't convinced for a moment. He was rich and gorgeous and successful and she was convinced that he had traversed a school of hard knocks to reach his current level. Cyrus had claimed that Nikolai's parents were a drug dealer and a whore and Ella knew no polite or gentle way of asking if that was the truth. What she did know was that sometimes Nikolai made her just want to hug him, and when he wasn't around it was a little like the sun vanishing without warning. She didn't understand how he could possibly have come to mean so much to her so quickly but there it was: Nikolai Drakos was already of enormous importance to her.

'I would want children,' Ella declared abruptly.

His dark head whipped up, caramel eyes flashing with surprise.

'And why are you looking surprised?' Ella enquired. 'Most women want children. I'm not talking this year or next year because I have to finish my training first, but eventually I would want children... I believe in being honest.'

Eventually.

'I've never wanted children,' Nikolai confessed.

'Well, it's children and me or *no* me, I'm afraid. Plus you'd also probably have to share your home with a selection of stray dogs and cats. That's probably not negotiable either,' Ella volunteered, determined to give him all the bad news at once before she lost her nerve and started trying to be someone she wasn't.

None of those life-changing possibilities was going to happen overnight, Nikolai reminded himself. She was trampling all over his most cherished convictions because she assumed that they would stay married for ever. But, of course, it wouldn't be that way, he reflected wryly. She would return to uni and meet some animal-loving younger man in muddy wellington boots and realise that Nikolai wasn't, after all, what she wanted. And he would let her go. A hollow sensation formed inside him. He pictured her in a country house awash with dogs and children. Home and family would come first with her...*always.* He understood that about her without even thinking about it. He couldn't give those things to her because he didn't form attachments, but she still deserved to have those things as well as the love of a man who deserved her.

'Are kids really a deal-breaker?' Ella demanded, troubled by the shadowed look on his lean, darkly handsome features. 'What *are* you thinking about?'

Nikolai sprang upright, bent down and scooped her off her seat to hold in his lap. 'Private matters.'

'If you marry me, you won't get to be private,' she warned him.

'Children aren't a deal-breaker if you're talking a couple of years down the road,' Nikolai conceded.

'And what if we have an accident?'

'I'm careful.'

Ella rested back in the cradle of his arms, drinking in the scent of his expensive cologne and the unique aroma that was purely, sexily his own. 'You really want to keep me?'

Nikolai screened his eyes. He knew that if a younger man in wellington boots had presented himself at that moment, he would have kicked him down the stairs and jumped on his corpse. He wanted her. He wanted her far more than he was comfortable with but he was equally aware of his guilt and of what he ought to be feeling. He had to be unselfish for *her* sake. 'I'll make you happy, *glikia mou*,' he swore doggedly and he meant every word of it.

He would make her happy, whatever it took and regardless of what it cost him. He would walk away from the pursuit of revenge that had consumed his life for the past five years. He would turn his back on Cyrus and his crimes for ever. Ella would become his first, his *only* priority.

'I believe you could,' Ella admitted in a softer tone than usual.

She wanted more time with him. She wanted to *be* with him because her heart stuttered and almost stopped at the thought of being without Nikolai. It was a visceral feeling, a scarily powerful feeling and not something she understood. She only understood that she needed to be with Nikolai. And there was a lot to be said in favour of a man who simply wanted to get married quickly, she reflected ruefully. Ella, after all, had been engaged for years to a man who had always found an excuse for not setting a wedding date. Paul had liked to talk about getting married but talking was as far as they had got.

'Yes, I'll marry you,' Ella declared with a sudden radiant smile.

Nikolai kissed her and a sizzle of naked longing snaked through her, leaving her limp and breathless. He settled her back down into her chair and produced a ring box while she looked on in astonishment.

'You have a ring?'

'Can't propose without a ring,' Nikolai quipped, sliding a diamond cluster onto her finger.

'It's dazzling,' she whispered as the diamonds flashed with iridescence in the sunshine. 'Thank you…'

'I'll stay in my apartment until the wedding,' Nikolai told her.

Ella gave him a bemused appraisal. 'But why?'

'I want to draw a strong line between where we started out and how we will continue,' Nikolai admitted smoothly. 'Everything will be different when we're married.'

* * *

'Nik's arranging for me to meet an interior designer here at the house next week,' Ella told Max when he served her breakfast two days later. 'I want the family things like photographs and papers put away somewhere safe first so that none of it ends up accidentally binned. I do think that at some stage Nik will want to look through it all. Where do you think we should start?'

'The late Mr Drakos's desk in the library. He kept a lot of stuff where he worked,' he volunteered. 'I'll try to get round every room before I leave.'

Ella frowned. *'Leave?'* she queried. 'Where are you going? Are you off on holiday or something?'

Max's thin face stiffened. 'I'm being replaced, Miss Palmer. Quite understandably your future husband has little faith in the man who allowed Cyrus Makris to enter his home.'

Max had been sacked over that? Ella was aghast at the news and furious that Nikolai had not told her about that decision. 'But that wasn't your fault... I mean, what happened.'

'What happened *happened*,' the older man pointed out with wry emphasis. 'I made a bad decision and you got hurt. Let's not discuss this, Miss Palmer. I not only let the man in but also went out leaving you alone with him.'

Angry words and defences bubbled in Ella's chest but she swallowed them back, recognising that further comment would only embarrass the older man. No, this was a matter she needed to take up directly with Nikolai. 'Could you give me directions to Nikolai's office?' she asked without hesitation. 'And perhaps while I'm out you could make a start on boxing up the Drakos family things I mentioned. If there are any particular pieces of furniture or other items that you feel should be considered an heirloom, please show them to me.'

Having lost the appetite to eat any more, Ella stood up. 'I'll fetch my bag.'

'Your driver will be waiting outside for you.'

'My...*driver*?'

'Mr Drakos has put a car and driver at your disposal...as well as a bodyguard,' Max completed. 'He wants to be assured of your safety twenty-four-seven.'

Ella shook her head in wonderment and compressed her lips. A driver? A bodyguard? Had Nikolai lost his wits? She was an ordinary woman and she did not require anyone to either drive her or guard her. He should have discussed those arrangements with her long before he made them.

Nikolai's offices were in a towering glass and steel office building that bore a fancy Drakos logo that appeared to be a dragon. Or was it a winged goddess like Nikolai's tattoo? She hadn't had the opportunity to get a closer look at it. To do that she would have to get his shirt off again. A rueful light entered her green eyes and her face warmed as she stood in the lift flanked by her silent monolith of a bodyguard, John. John was quiet to the extent that had he not cast such a big shadow she might almost have been able to forget he was there.

In Reception she asked to see Nikolai and was told he was in a meeting. Ignoring the fact, she sat down to wait and sent him a text warning him that she *had* to speak to him. Thirty minutes passed slowly and then a svelte older woman approached her to take her to him.

'You can wait for me here,' she told her bodyguard.

She smoothed down her fine wool trousers and the cashmere jacket that, in concert with her stiletto-heeled boots, gave her a fashionable air. Now that she wore Nikolai's ring she had no qualms about wearing the clothes he had bought her. It felt right, just as it had felt right to call Gramma and her father and share her wedding news and smile at their happiness on her behalf. Yet below the smile lurked a deep well of insecurity, for there were certain facts she could not ignore. She hadn't known Nikolai for very long and she knew very little about him because he was not the kind of male who shared personal details. Yet here she was, preparing to confront him over what she deemed to be a very bad decision.

'I have a bone to pick with you,' she murmured the instant she stepped into his office.

Without visible reaction, Nikolai studied her with shrewd dark eyes. 'That doesn't sound promising. I like the boots though.'

'Of course you do,' Ella groaned. 'Men always like sexy boots. You're being predictable. But when you sacked Max, you were being a complete tyrant... I don't want to marry a tyrant, Nikolai!'

An angry frown slowly drew together his black brows. 'He complained to you?'

'No, he didn't. I found out...quite by accident actually,' she assured him defensively. 'Can't you see that you're being unjust? Did you ever tell Max not to let Cyrus into your home?'

'No,' Nikolai conceded grudgingly.

'Well, then, how can you blame Max for what happened? *I* greeted Cyrus. Max knew that he was my visitor and thought nothing of it,' Ella protested.

'Max put you at risk. I can't close my eyes to that and whether I hire or fire anyone I employ is not your business,' he completed in a tone of cold finality.

Ella was undaunted, her eyes gleaming like polished emeralds. 'Oh, I would think that the hiring or firing of staff in the marital home would be very much my business as your wife.'

'But at present it is not our marital home and you are not my wife as yet,' Nikolai pointed out in stubborn challenge. 'The responsibility remains mine.'

'If you want it to *be* our marital home and you want me to *be* your wife you will listen to me,' Ella told him in raw frustration. 'You're being unfair to Max. I hadn't the faintest idea that Cyrus was liable to turn violent like that, so how was Max supposed to know? How were any of us supposed to know that?'

And that was the crux of the matter, Nikolai reflected with bitter acceptance. Everything that had happened was *his* fault. Only he had known that Cyrus could be dangerous. He had never dreamt, though, that Cyrus would dare to approach Ella when she was staying with Nikolai. But then very probably Cyrus had heard about the hotel fire and had assumed that that particular morning Nikolai would be otherwise engaged. Nikolai knew that he should have warned Max never to let Cyrus Makris into his home but that possibility hadn't even crossed his mind. When he had realised that Cyrus was there, when he had found Cyrus attacking Ella, the world had turned blood red for Nikolai. He knew that if Ella had not intervened, he would have kept on hitting Cyrus and in the aftermath he had been looking for someone to blame for an untenable situation. Someone, *anyone* other than his own self, he acknowledged with a fierce regret that he could never have expressed.

In the smouldering silence, Ella studied Nikolai. She knew he was thinking hard and fast and deep but typically he was not sharing a single thought. 'You said you wanted to make me happy. I *like* Max. You were exhausted that day after the fire. That ghastly episode with Cyrus upset you more. Don't make Max carry the can for something that wasn't his fault.'

'If I'm in the wrong I will change my decision,' Nikolai declared in a driven undertone.

'And why have I suddenly got a driver and a body-guard the size of a mountain?'

Nikolai breathed in slow and deep and wondered if this was what marriage promised to be like. Would Ella challenge his every decision? He made his own choices and he always stood by them but suddenly he was being faced with the need to compromise, the need to defend or reconsider his black-and-white thinking processes. It would be a steep challenge to become less rigid and more flexible for her sake.

Making Ella happy and keeping her happy would be no cake walk.

'I won't apologise for hiring a bodyguard for your benefit. It is my responsibility to keep you safe and I take it very seriously,' Nikolai assured her confidently. 'I will not take the risk of Cyrus approaching you again.'

'Do you really think that is likely?' Ella pressed in astonishment.

'He was off his head with rage that day. I don't think that we can afford to assume that he will keep his distance. I prefer to ensure that you are protected when I'm not around.'

Ella searched his lean, hard features and the lack of compromise etched in his strong bone structure. She suppressed a sigh.

'I will consider retaining Max but I will not reconsider my decision to hire a driver and a bodyguard,' Nikolai admitted with flat emphasis. 'Quit while you're ahead, Ella.'

'We still have so much to learn about each other,' Ella whispered ruefully. 'Am I stressing you out?'

His dark golden eyes glittered. 'I have strong shoulders.'

Nikolai was all male as he stood there straight and tall and tough. He wasn't about to admit that he had made a mistake with Max but she knew she had won because Nikolai had a strong streak of fairness. But in pushing that issue, she had crossed a line with Nikolai and she recognised that as well. She had forced him to acknowledge her as an equal, not as a weak or lesser person, and he wouldn't forget that.

Nikolai surveyed her, his wide sensual lips set in a hard line. He would take no risks with her safety and he didn't care if that infringed her freedom. If anything happened to her he would never forgive himself. She was *his* to look after. Only a couple of weeks back he hadn't recognised the level of responsibility he was taking on by bringing her into his life but he did now.

Ella first, second and third…by the time she met a nice young man in welly boots he would probably be relieved to graciously step back and hand her over. At least that was supposed to be his real goal, Nikolai conceded with brooding ferocity. Familiarity was supposed to lead to contempt. Responsibility was supposed to make a man long for freedom. If she met another man, would he then return to normal?

He was grimly conscious that in some peculiar way he had changed from the moment he saw Ella again. His legendary cool control was under attack. His mind was no longer his own. Ella sneaked into his thoughts far more often than was reasonable and he was already regretting having loftily declared that they would live apart until the wedding.

Indeed, so disturbing were the changes that he recognised in himself that he felt almost at the mercy of reactions and thoughts and anxieties that he had suppressed for years. That slight hint of instability totally unnerved him and made him feel like a man on the edge of a precipice. Even worse, the threat of seeing Ella with another man clenched every muscle in his body with aggression. Right at this very moment he knew he couldn't face that possibility, but surely with time those responses would fade?

It would be so simple. He would get used to having her around. He would get bored; *she* would get bored. She would want her freedom back and he would let her go…*wouldn't he*?

CHAPTER EIGHT

'So, ARE YOU putting in a replacement now?' Ella prompted the nurse who was engaged in removing the old contraceptive implant from her arm.

'Dr Jenks only asked me to remove this one,' the older woman responded cagily.

Perhaps her doctor thought she was suffering side effects from the implant, Ella reasoned wryly. That would mean looking at other contraceptive methods. Hopefully one without side effects, she thought ruefully, because she had only come to see the doctor in the first place because she wasn't feeling herself. Not ill exactly, just not *right*. Her appetite had changed, her taste buds had gone awry and she was suddenly so blasted tired all the time! He had sent her for a battery of tests the day before and made a second appointment for her.

Ella was grateful she had come home, which had enabled her to see her usual doctor rather than having to find a new one in London. She had persuaded Nikolai that she wanted to be married from home, so that family and friends could easily attend, and tomorrow was the big day. She still couldn't quite believe it but there was something that felt very right about the real-

ity that she literally couldn't wait to get down the aisle
to become Nikolai's wife.

'It's called love,' Gramma had told her cheerfully.
'I'd have been worried if you weren't excited about getting married to him.'

Resisting the urge to rub her slightly sore arm with
its neat little plaster, Ella returned to the doctor's surgery. She was thinking about her wedding dress, which
she adored, when one of the doctor's measured words
finally penetrated her wandering concentration. Conceived…*conceived*? Her mind went blank as though
the word were foreign because the very unexpected-
ness of it threw rationality out of the window.

'But I had the implant!' she bleated, hands abruptly
closing very tightly together on her lap.

'As I pointed out, the implant is only effective for
three years and you missed your follow-up appointment
and failed to respond to the letter that was sent out.'

'But it *is* only three years since—' she began heatedly.

Dr Jenks went through the dates with her. In fact,
it turned out to be over four years since she had got
the implant and she had the vaguest recollection of the
reminder letter he mentioned. After Paul had passed
away, contraception had been very low on the list of
her priorities. But Ella was still stunned to appreciate
that when she had lost her virginity with Nikolai she
had not been protected as she had naively assumed. Her
main mistake had been the assumption that the implant
lasted for four years when in fact it only worked for
three. And she *had* conceived. Nikolai was going to
be shattered…but Ella was equally convinced that she
would never recover from the shock either.

Until that moment Ella had believed that total honesty between partners was the only way to go. And then without the smallest warning, she found herself changing her mind. Floating down the aisle to Nikolai and announcing almost simultaneously that she was pregnant would absolutely ruin the day. He would be taken aback, unprepared, *stressed out* by the news because Nikolai was a planner, who liked everything in its place, everything clean and tidy. And there was nothing clean or tidy about an unplanned pregnancy when they would be only newly married and looking forward to the unfettered joys of coupledom. In addition he had been quite blunt about only wanting to become a parent in a few years' time.

They were flying to Crete after the wedding to stay at the house Nikolai owned there. She would tell him on the island, when he was relaxed and better able to handle an unforeseen development. *Pregnant!* Ella drove back home and reflected that her own mother must have suffered a similar shock when she realised that she was pregnant. Ella, after all, had not been a planned baby either and her arrival had threatened to derail her mother's career plans. Soon after her birth, however, her mother had flown off to take up her top job, leaving her infant daughter behind with her father and grandmother. To walk away had been her choice. What if Nikolai felt so strongly about not starting a family that he chose to walk away too? No, that was the absolute worst-case scenario, Ella told herself firmly. He had said that he was willing to have a family eventually and there was nothing wrong with holding back on telling him her news. It wasn't as though she would be telling him any lies, she was simply *delaying* telling him, she reasoned defensively.

Ella knew that once again her own plans would be forced back on hold because it would be incredibly difficult for her to adequately complete her training while she was pregnant. But she knew too that sometimes it was necessary to make the best one could of a life change that came as a surprise. It would only be a bad development if she allowed herself to think that it was. All right, she conceded, the timing wasn't what she would have chosen but she had always wanted children. She thought of all the worse things that could have happened, imagining how she would have felt had she had trouble conceiving, and before very long her dismay subsided entirely. As for Nikolai? She would wrap up her news like the gift she believed it to be and present it to him at the best possible moment.

'You look so beautiful,' Gramma enthused warmly as Ella twirled at the foot of the stairs.

Her father was misty-eyed at the picture his daughter made in her lace wedding gown. The gorgeous lace was her only adornment because Ella, conscious of her diminutive height, had opted for a plain design that bared only her back while encasing her arms and slender body in sleek lace. On her feet she rocked a considerably less conservative set of strappy, very high-heeled lace ankle boots, teamed with stockings and a garter. Nikolai liked boots and Ella was in the mood to give her bridegroom boots.

She hadn't breathed a word about her pregnancy since she left the surgery. She felt that announcement should first be heard by her baby's father. They trav-

elled to the little local church in the limo Nikolai had
sent, her bodyguard bringing up the rear in his own
vehicle. The church was full and she walked down the
aisle slowly on her father's arm, noting all the unfamiliar faces on Nikolai's side of the church and thinking
it sad that he had not a single relative to grace those
pews. She had, however, from the letters and cards she
had found in the town house, discovered that Nikolai's
grandfather had twin sisters still living on the island
of Crete, where the Drakos family had originated, and
she wondered if Nikolai would make use of that information.

Nikolai watched his bride approach with bated
breath. His brain told him there was no such thing as
perfection but he *saw* only perfection, from the sleek
coil of Ella's bronze hair to the fine-tuned delicacy
of her figure encased in exquisite lace. It had been
less than a week since he had seen her but it felt like
a lot longer. *Thee mou*, he couldn't sleep for wanting
her and, as he had so frequently told himself, getting
married meant an end to cold showers and wondering where she was, who she might be with and what
she was doing. He watched her drift towards him with
keenly appreciative eyes of possession and pride.

Ella smiled at the altar, looking up into those melted-
caramel eyes, admiring the smooth angle of his strong
jawline, the jut of his nose and the high cheekbones
that lent his lean, darkly handsome features such electrifying magnetism. The ring went onto her finger and
she thought about the baby with a deep inner sense of
happiness. Since she had found out so early it would
be ages until she started showing and she had plenty of

time before she needed to worry about telling Nikolai that he was going to be a father.

They travelled to the hotel where the reception was being staged. 'You have a lot of friends,' she remarked.

'Mostly business acquaintances,' he corrected. 'While you seem to have hundreds of cousins.'

'Dad has five sisters,' she reminded him.

'My very best wishes. I'm Marika Makris, Cyrus's sister.' A middle-aged brunette wearing a superb diamond necklace introduced herself to Ella while the bridal couple circulated amongst their guests before the wedding breakfast was served. Nikolai had mentioned in passing that Marika would be attending and she knew that the older woman had been estranged from her brother for years, so there should be nothing uncomfortable about the meeting.

'Ella… Drakos,' Ella framed and laughed. 'It's so hard to say a different name but Nikolai very much wanted me to take his name.'

'Naturally, you *are* Nikolai's crowning triumph,' Marika informed her with a smug little smile.

'Well…thank you,' Ella responded after a blank pause in which no inspiration came to mind.

'Nikolai and Cyrus have been enemies for so long that my brother forgot to watch his back,' the brunette remarked sagely before drifting on at a regal pace.

Ella blinked in bewilderment. Enemies? Since when had Nikolai and Cyrus been enemies? She knew they didn't get on, but thought they were just business rivals. But enemies spoke of something much deeper between them. Both men were Greek, which she supposed was the connection. Resolving to ask Nikolai about that comment later, she took her seat for the meal.

After eating, she went to the cloakroom to repair her make-up. As she paused at a crowded corner to allow people to pass her by she heard a woman say loudly, 'What I want to know is what does *she* have that the rest of us don't? Nikolai is the original ice man and he ditched all of us in record time!'

Ella's brows rose. 'Ditched *all* of us?' Who was she eavesdropping on? The ex-girlfriends' club?

'She *is* beautiful,' another female voice opined regretfully.

'She's the size of a shrimp!' someone else objected. 'But she must have some very special quality for him to be marrying her.'

'Maybe she's a wildcat in bed,' the first voice suggested.

'Maybe he's finally fallen in love,' the kinder voice that had described Ella as beautiful remarked.

There was an outbreak of female voices at that point. 'If pigs could fly!' was one of the few repeatable opinions expressed.

Lifting her chin and gathering her pride, Ella rounded the corner and passed the small group of fashionably dressed women all waving glasses around and talking loudly. Even a cursory glance in their direction was sufficient to warn her that Nikolai had very good taste and while Nikolai had apparently dumped those women they were all attending the wedding with partners. How naive she had been not to be prepared for the reality that Nikolai was almost certain to have former lovers attending, she thought wryly.

She studied herself in the mirror. A shrimp? Well, compared to those tall, shapely ladies outside she was indeed a shrimp in size, she conceded ruefully. Seem-

ingly Nikolai had once had a particular type he went
for because all those women were blonde. So where
did she fit in? And why had he married her? She could
not help recalling Cyrus's claim that Nikolai was noto-
riously badly behaved with women. Possibly that had
been true, Ella reasoned, but people could change…
couldn't they?

'You're as stiff as a fence post,' Nikolai groaned as
they opened the dancing, something Ella was not very
confident about doing in front of an audience. 'And
you're very quiet. Naturally I'm worried.'

'How many ex-girlfriends of yours are here today?'

His wide shoulders tensed. 'A couple, and only because they're now married to friends of mine. Why?
Has someone said something they shouldn't?'

'Don't talk down to me like I'm a child!' Ella
snapped into his chest, feeling distinctly shrimp-like
in spite of her heels.

'If you won't tell me what's wrong there's nothing
I can do about it.'

'There's nothing wrong,' Ella declared loftily, drinking in the scent of his cologne and the husky, intrin-
sic smell that was purely him and which warmed her
somewhere down deep inside. There was no way on
earth she was about to allow insecurity to drive her
into arguing with him on their wedding day. 'But be
warned. I'm the jealous type. And I may be small but
I'm lethal.'

'I knew that already,' Nikolai confessed, long fingers splaying caressingly across her bare spine as he
shifted his lithe hips against her. 'Lethally appealing
and lethally sexy.'

'Wait until you see the boots,' she whispered teasingly, wildly aware of his arousal and flattered that he was in that state purely because he was close to her. 'And the garter and the stockings.'

'I'm getting you in stockings for my wedding night?' Nikolai murmured thickly. 'Bring it on, *khriso mou*!'

And Ella laughed and forgot about what she had overheard. Of course he had exes and a past but that was life and she had to live with it.

'I felt sad when I realised that you didn't have a single relative at our wedding,' Ella admitted during the flight in the private jet to Crete.

'I didn't feel sad,' Nikolai countered squarely, lounging back in his leather seat, very much in command. 'But then I didn't have a white-picket-fence childhood like yours.'

'It wasn't like that. I didn't have a mother,' Ella argued and shared her story.

'You had a father and a grandmother who loved you. You were lucky.'

But Ella would never forget how rejected she had felt when she had first met her mother as a teenager. Her mother had not regretted never having got to know her and, more hurtfully still, had had no ambition to foster an adult friendship with her long-lost daughter either. It had been a one-off meeting and a disappointment. In truth it had made Ella better appreciate the family she did have.

'Family can be toxic,' Nikolai remarked with rich cynicism.

'How...*toxic*?' she questioned uncertainly. 'Tell me about your childhood.'

'It's ugly.'

'I can handle ugly. Tell me about your father.'

Nikolai grimaced. 'He got into trouble from an early age. He was thrown out of several schools for dealing in drugs,' he divulged.

'How did you find that out?'

'My grandfather's solicitor told me what he knew about my background when he was trying to explain why the old man was so determined not to meet me,' Nikolai explained with a wry twist of his expressive mouth. 'Although my father was given every support to turn his life around and numerous second chances he continually chose to return to crime and violence.'

'Some people are just born with that tendency,' Ella imputed, sadness gripping her that Nikolai could not even respect his father's memory. No son would want such a father and nor would he want to grow up in such a man's image. 'What about your mother?'

'She was Russian…a lap dancer called Natalya.'

'You're half Russian?' Ella cut in, her surprise unhidden.

'When Natalya became pregnant with my sister, my father married her. Possibly the only conventional thing he ever did in his life. At some stage my grandfather disinherited him and cut off all contact with him. I have few memories before the age of five,' Nikolai admitted stiffly. 'I do remember chaos…shouts, screams, hiding behind a locked door with my sister begging me to keep quiet. My father was in and out of prison. We moved around a lot. There were frequent police raids, gang attacks. My sister looked after me.'

Ella was quietly appalled by what she was learning about his background and finally comprehending why

Nikolai would say that a family could be toxic. 'Why not your mother? Was she at work?'

'No, she didn't work. She was always in the background somewhere drunk or high. But for Sofia I would either have starved or been beaten to death. My father took his frustrations out on me,' Nikolai volunteered without any expression at all, watching her as though he was measuring her reactions to what he was telling her, which made her all the more careful not to reveal a sympathy, which could hurt his pride. 'He broke Sofia's nose once when she came between us in an effort to protect me... I was more her child than my mother's.'

'I'm really sorry it was so bad for you,' Ella whispered, green eyes luminous with a compassion she couldn't hide.

She wondered if anyone but his sister had ever loved Nikolai. And he had lost her as well. Was that why he kept himself so isolated? Why he was so determinedly detached?

'My parents died in a car crash when I was ten and my grandfather set up a trust to pay for my education. I was sent straight to boarding school in England.'

'He saved every one of your school reports,' Ella reminded him, because she had told him what she had found in his grandfather's desk. 'And yet he didn't want to meet you?'

'He was afraid of being disappointed. I think he'd already worked out by then that if you make an emotional investment in individuals you get hurt, and he was old and tired.'

'So, he kept you at arm's length.' Ella sighed. 'But he missed out on so much. Obviously you're not like your father.'

'I'm brighter but I don't know that I'm better,' Nikolai murmured with forbidding honesty, studying her in all her bridal finery. So appealing and beautiful, so vulnerable, so *clean*. She had probably never done a really mean thing in her life. Ella was too good for him. He knew that he didn't deserve her. He had seduced her with blackmail into his bed...no honour or decency there! And if she knew him now as he truly was and stripped of pretence, she would never have married him.

'Your troubled background was what made you... unsure about having a family, wasn't it?' Ella probed helplessly.

Nikolai shrugged a broad shoulder. 'Of course. What does a man like me know about being part of a normal family? How could I ever be a father when I wouldn't know where to begin?'

Ella paled. 'You could learn.'

'And what if I don't have the interest to learn? I've heard that children put a lot of pressure on a relationship. Why would you take that risk?' Nikolai enquired with sardonic bite.

Ella could only think of the tiny seed in her womb, which she would have protected with her life, and she turned her head away lest her face reveal too much. For the first time she was scared of what she had to tell Nikolai. It was true that, while he had no experience of family life, he could certainly learn. But would he *want* to learn? A baby coming so early in their marriage would definitely impose restrictions on them that he might well resent. Yet it was important to Ella that her baby have two loving parents, for she knew how much her own mother's indifference had hurt her even as a young adult.

'And I'm not *unsure* about whether or not to have children,' Nikolai contradicted. 'I have simply never felt the need to reproduce.'

'But you *agreed* that if I—' she began heatedly.

'Yes. I'm not that selfish. I will adapt to whatever the future brings.'

But how far would 'adapting' get him if he had a fundamental dislike of the idea of becoming a parent? Ella repressed the thought and breathed in deep and slow. She had to be patient and understanding, not critical and pushy. Honey was much more effective than vinegar.

She collided with hard dark eyes, finally noticing the rigidity of his sculpted bone structure. Nikolai's sheer tension leapt out at her. She had raised sensitive issues when she'd forced him to share the story of his dysfunctional childhood and family. Was it any wonder he was on the defensive? Still gorgeous though, no matter what mood he was in, she thought helplessly as she studied him, her guilty conscience assailing her until the germ of a wild idea struck her. The instant she thought of it she wanted to smash the mould of his undoubtedly low expectations and seduce him.

Could she? *Dared* she? Wasn't this the male who had moved heaven and earth to bring her into his life and his bed? With Nikolai she never needed to doubt her welcome. Nikolai always wanted her. Uplifted by that conviction, she felt bold but she also needed to be closer to him and she craved the soothing balm of the intense connection they shared when they made love. Unclipping her seat belt, she stood up before she could lose her nerve. 'Ask the cabin staff to stay out,' she told him tightly.

His brow indented as he lifted the phone at his elbow and spoke. He stared at her, watching the colour rise in her cheeks. 'Why?'

'Newly married? Do not disturb? Do I need to draw a picture?' she asked teasingly, feeling the wanton heat of anticipation coil at the heart of her.

'I think perhaps you do,' Nikolai murmured, still frowning, still not getting the message.

Ella tugged up the tight skirt of her gown and knelt very deliberately down at his feet and pressed his thighs apart. Only as she reached for his belt buckle did the extreme tension go out of him to be replaced by tension of an entirely different variety.

'You're kidding me?' Nikolai husked, black lashes rising over stunned dark eyes.

'Does this feel like a wind-up?' Ella enquired, running a caressing palm down over the revealing bulge at his groin.

He shivered, hard dark eyes flashing to pools of melted-caramel astonishment.

Face hot, Ella ran down his zip. Helpfully he lifted his hips to allow her to move his pants out of the way. She was determined to use all the things that she had learnt from the books she had read. Her tongue stole a long swipe along the length of him.

Nikolai swore in Greek and pushed back in his seat with a little groan. 'I never know what to expect from you but I adore the way you continually surprise me. Presumably you know what you're doing...'

'No, this technique is straight out of a book.'

'A *book*?' he repeated in disbelief.

'Shut up…you're distracting me,' she muttered shakily, settling down to practise everything she had learned with enthusiasm.

Nikolai very quickly decided that she must've read a humdinger of a text. Her tongue stroked and flicked and circled and her luscious lips engulfed. Her warm, wet mouth took him to paradise. His hands fisted in her hair and as she found her rhythm an earthy groan of satisfaction escaped him. She looked up at him once when he was right on the edge, little shudders travelling through his muscular thighs, eyes glowing gold.

Nikolai had never been so aroused and he knew he wouldn't last long. He tried to back off once he realised he was about to come but she wouldn't let him take control. He climaxed in a storm of raw excitement and threw his dark head back, watching in wonderment as his so recently virginal bride swallowed, zipped him back up, straightened her dress and returned to her seat as though nothing had happened.

'A book?' Nikolai queried raggedly as he shifted with voluptuous contentment in his seat.

'Why not a book? I don't like not knowing how to do things.'

'I'm willing to teach you anything you ask, *so* willing,' Nikolai savoured in a roughened undertone, still barely able to credit what she had just done. 'You are insanely sexy, *khriso mou*. I am a very lucky man.'

Ella was so pleased that she'd chased the shadows away. His eyes had been haunted because she had asked him to talk about his disturbing childhood, but she had sent his thoughts and his imagination racing in a far more positive direction. There was more she needed to know about Nikolai's past, but she had learnt enough for the present and she loved him. Loved him so much that she couldn't bear to see shadows in his lean dark face and listen to him insisting that he wasn't sensitive or upset when he *was*.

And she had learned from what he had told her as well. One person had rejected her but more than one had rejected Nikolai: his mother, his father, his grandfather. Of course he didn't know how a family operated. Of course he worried about being a father when his own had set such a bad example. But with her love and support his outlook would change so that when he found out about their baby he would feel very differently...wouldn't he?

CHAPTER NINE

'So, WHERE ARE we staying?' Ella enquired after a car had collected them from Heraklion Airport and begun the drive along the coastal road in the fading light of dusk.

'The house where my grandfather was born.'

'I like a place with family connections,' Ella admitted. 'Did you inherit it?'

'Yes, but by the time I did it hadn't been occupied in years and it needed gutting. It started out as a simple farmhouse, which was gentrified when the family fortunes improved, but my grandfather never used it. I almost had it demolished,' he confided with a wry smile. 'And then I stood on the veranda in the sunlight and thought of all the generations who must have enjoyed that same view and I decided to try and retain the character of the place.'

'You see, you *do* have sentimental attachments,' Ella told him with an appreciative glance as the car turned off the main road onto a much more narrow one lined with trees.

'I also have a surprise for you,' Nikolai admitted. 'But you won't get it until later.'

The house was larger than she had expected, a

sprawling ranch-style villa with various offshoots and a large inviting veranda. Nikolai gave her a brief tour of the house, which was all cool tiled floors and contemporary furnishings. The beautifully carved staircase had been conserved, as had a turn-of-the-century stained-glass window of saints in the hall, but it remained first and foremost a luxurious and comfortable modern home.

At the foot of the stairs, Nikolai bent without warning and scooped her up into his arms.

'What on earth?' Ella gasped.

'I always wanted a woman small enough to carry up the stairs.'

'So why did you only get involved with very tall blondes?' Ella quipped, unimpressed, thinking about the women she had heard talking about him at the wedding.

'I was running scared,' Nikolai assured her, deadpan. 'I knew when I found a little one I'd have to marry her.'

Involuntarily, Ella laughed because he was so slick with that response. He pressed open the door on a spacious bedroom. A tall geometric vase of glorious flowers adorned a side table and beside it stood an ice bucket and two champagne flutes. He lowered her carefully to the polished wood floor and uncorked the champagne to fill the glasses. Ella put the glass to her lips, bubbles breaking beneath her nose as she pretended to sip as she had done all day while drinks were served and toasts were being made.

'You look fantastic in that dress,' he told her huskily, sincerity ringing from every syllable and empowering her.

Ella set her flute down and turned her back to him. 'Undo my hooks,' she urged.

'You're still determined to surprise me,' he said thickly, deftly dealing with the hooks at her nape and then running down the side zip over the swell of her hips.

Ella moved back a few steps, loosening her sleeves and slowly working the gown down and off, murderously conscious of the bareness of her breasts because the dress had had built-in support. And she was still shy with him, foolish she knew after the intimacy they had already shared but she was still afraid that he might be disappointed by what she had to offer.

Nikolai leant back against the ornate black iron footboard on the bed and stared at her. 'I think I've died and gone to heaven, *khriso mou.*'

Fiercely resisting the urge to cover her breasts with her hands, Ella stepped out of the gown and settled it over a chair.

Nikolai simply gloried in the view. She was wearing ridiculously cute lace ankle boots and stockings that stopped mid-thigh. One slender thigh sported a frilly blue garter and cream lace knickers encased her pert little derriere. Breasts with straining soft pink nipples seized his attention and that fast he was on sexual fire.

Ella loved that Nikolai was staring at her like a man in the grip of a holy vision. He made her feel like a sex goddess. Suddenly it didn't matter that she had tiny boobs and a rail-thin body. Nikolai looking at her like that was like a shot of power-packed adrenalin in her veins. He peeled off his jacket, wrenched almost clumsily at his shirt. A long delicious slice of bronzed muscular torso appeared.

'And the best thing of all, *khriso mou*,' he breathed in a roughened undertone as he reached for her. 'That ring on your finger says you're all mine.'

He fed on her mouth like a hungry wolf and that kiss was rough, uncompromising and absolutely dominant. It also set alight every nerve ending in her quivering body. He pushed her down on the bed and claimed a taut little nipple while long fingers toyed with its twin. It was as if an electrifying piece of elastic ran between her breasts and her pelvis as the heat surged through her. A finger skimmed aside her knickers and skated through her damp folds. As she gasped he groaned.

'You're so ready for me...' he savoured, claiming her succulent mouth again with driving hunger.

He spread her out on the bed like a pagan sacrifice and the burn at the heart of her tingled and seethed even before the stubble on his face grazed her inner thighs. She wanted him so much. She had never wanted anything or anybody so much that it literally hurt to wait. A finger teased her inner sheath and her hips wriggled, her spine arching as he found the tiny bundle of nerves with his expert mouth. And what happened after that, well, she wasn't quite sure because she was bucking and shifting and moaning and the pleasure kept on building and building until she couldn't contain it any more and a climax ripped through her lower body like a detonation, flaming through every limb and nerve ending with explosive effect. It was almost as though the world stopped for a moment and she held onto him as though he were a rock in a whirlwind.

'I love what you do to me,' she whispered breathlessly into a satin-smooth dark-skinned shoulder.

'That was a bit bull-in-a-china-shop,' Nikolai

growled, rolling free and springing off the bed, dark eyes volatile as a hot fire ready to rage out of control. 'This is our wedding night. It was supposed to be a slow, sweet seduction.'

'Stop talking,' Ella told him. 'Being thrown on the bed works for me. Seeing you a little out of control is more *real* than some plan of slow seduction.'

'Blame yourself. You've been wrecking my plans all day,' Nikolai asserted, swiping the package off the dressing table and returning to the bed. 'First you blew my mind on the flight and then you flaunted your gorgeous self in boots and stockings and a garter and I was *lost…*'

'Is that a complaint?'

'No.' A wicked charismatic grin slashed his lean, darkly handsome features. 'That was an "any time you want me, I'm yours" speech,' he teased.

'You can be yourself with me, you know,' she whispered feelingly. 'Just do what you feel like.'

'Can't,' Nikolai incised, passing her the package. 'I'd eat you alive. Happy wedding day, Mrs Drakos.'

'I didn't get you anything.'

'You gave me you…unforgettably,' Nikolai growled, flipping open the box for her in his impatience and lifting out a three-strand pearl necklace with an elaborate emerald and diamond clasp.

'My word…' Ella stroked a wondering finger over the gleaming iridescence of the perfect pearls. 'It's really beautiful.'

Nikolai clasped the necklace round her throat. 'Their purity reminded me of you.'

'I'm not pure… I'm not perfect…nobody needs to be perfect,' Ella declared in a rush, thinking of the secret she was holding within her body, fearing his reaction more than ever because, the happier she became, the more she feared a potential fall.

'You're a lot more pure and perfect than I will ever be.' Nikolai pushed the tangle of bronze-coloured hair back behind her small ears and tipped up her chin to kiss her again.

The heat inside her claimed her again faster than she could've believed. It was as though her body were programmed to his. A muscular, hair-roughened thigh slid between hers as he rested her back on the pillows again and everything below her waist tingled with awareness.

'I want you so much,' she whispered helplessly.

'And you're going to get me. Over and over and over again,' Nikolai husked hungrily against her swollen mouth.

Ella stroked the long, thick length of jutting virility against his stomach, no longer nervous, no longer unsure. He wanted her every bit as much as she wanted him and knowing that set her free and filled her with happiness.

'If you do that I won't last.'

Ella reared up and pushed him flat. 'Oh, stop with the threats, Mr Drakos!' she told him, laughing down at him.

Nikolai could never remember laughter along with sex but he liked it. He liked it even more when he pulled her back down again and reinstated supremacy because there was no way he would allow her to call the shots in bed. He felt strange, almost giddy, and he wanted to smile and he wondered what was wrong with him. His little hummingbird of a bride was changing him and he knew as he looked down into her hectically flushed, laughing face that there was no way he was ever going to willingly hand her over to another man.

'I want this night to last for ever,' she murmured against his chest, drunk on the smell of his skin.

'*For ever* is a big challenge,' he husked, rocking his hips against hers, letting her feel the hardness of him, sending a wanton thrill of naked hunger shooting through her veins.

'It wasn't a challenge,' she protested as he touched her where she most needed to be touched and she jerked and whimpered, defenceless against the surge of need controlling her.

He eased over her, rearranged her to his satisfaction, slowly surged in and she shut her eyes tight, every nerve screaming for the satisfaction only he could give. Inch by agonising inch he entered her and when he was finally fully seated she loosed a sound of pleasure she couldn't hold back. She could feel how damp, how ready she was and his sheer strength as he lifted her up to him, muscles bulging in his forearms, left her weak with longing. He slid back and then plunged, his speed picking up. Excitement detonated inside her and she wrapped her legs round him. As she bucked he pinned her to the mattress and thrust into her fiercely with a primal grunt of pleasure. It went on and on and on until she was sobbing with excitement and the band of tension at the centre of her body was tightening and tightening. Release came in a rush of feral fire, lighting up every nerve and skin cell, and she cried out, her nails raking down his back in an ecstasy of pleasure.

She was dizzy with lingering joy when she recovered enough to be aware of her surroundings again.

'I'm flattening you.' He dropped a gentle kiss on her brow and released her from his weight to turn over.

Flatten away, she almost told him, until her attention was grabbed by the tattoo on his shoulder. Yes, it was a winged goddess, but incongruously a tiny rainbow and the head of a unicorn peeked out from below one wing. 'A rainbow and a unicorn?' she queried, tracing the design with a curious fingertip.

Nikolai went rigid and flipped back to face her, dark eyes grim in his lean, strong face. 'To remember my sister...the fairy-tale things she liked,' he confided with a reluctance she could feel.

'That's sweet...when did she...?'

'Five years ago.' His rich, dark drawl had gone all gravelly. 'I don't want to discuss it.'

'OK,' Ella said lightly, although it wasn't OK in any way and his reserve hurt.

Did you really think being married to Nikolai was going to be all rainbows and unicorns? she asked herself irritably. He wasn't going to have a personality transplant overnight and suddenly begin sharing his every innermost thought and feeling. Obviously he still felt the loss of his sister deeply and he wasn't ready to talk about it yet. That was all right. She didn't have to blunder in where angels feared to tread, did she? She didn't have to know *everything* about him...did she?

Love was a hard taskmaster, she conceded then, running a tender fingertip over the hard line of his tense mouth before giving up on that approach and rolling away from him to climb off the bed. 'I'm still wearing my boots,' she noted in wonderment.

'I like them,' Nikolai told her in a driven undertone.

'I knew you would...but my feet are hurting now,'

she admitted, sitting down by the table with the flowers to take the boots off and noticing the envelope sitting there unopened. 'Oh, you haven't opened this yet. It must be from whoever sent the flowers.'

Sitting up in the bed, Nikolai tensed again as she dug out the card. 'Dido and Dorkas Drakos…the flowers are from your great-aunts!' Ella exclaimed with satisfaction. 'You'll have to go and look them up now.'

'I hate to rain on your parade but I met them years ago when I was having this place renovated,' Nikolai admitted abruptly.

'You didn't mention that,' she said in surprise. 'Were they friendly?'

'Very…but it seemed a bit too late in the day to get sucked into the family circle when I had spent most of my life alone,' he admitted stiffly.

'When did they first find out that you existed?' she pressed.

'When I inherited from my grandfather.'

'Then you can't blame them for not being around when you were younger,' Ella pointed out squarely. 'We should go and visit…see how it goes.'

Nikolai rolled his eyes and said nothing. Meeting his relatives would make her happy and it would cost him nothing. He knew she was keen to give him family roots on Crete. She couldn't grasp that he had lived most of his life without such ties and that they meant a great deal less to him than they did to her. He had learned a lot in his first ten years at the hands of totally detached parents.

A little hurt by his discouraging silence, Ella went for a shower. As she stepped out of the cubicle, however, he stepped in.

'Do you want some supper?' Nikolai enquired when he wandered back into the bedroom clad in the twin of the dark towelling robe she had found hanging in the bathroom.

'Is there anything available?' Ella asked, knowing that he wasn't much better at cooking than she was. At home she had looked after her father when he'd needed care and had generally taken over his jobs, keeping the garden and lighting the fire, while Gramma had presided over the kitchen. There had never been any need for Ella to learn how to cook.

Nikolai gave her an amused appraisal. 'I think you'll be pleasantly surprised.'

Ella was bemused when she heard dogs barking somewhere nearby. Nikolai opened the bedroom door and Rory and Butch charged in to careen round his feet. He moved the vase of flowers to allow Max to settle a laden tray down on the table.

'This was my surprise,' Nikolai told her wryly.

'I thought it was the pearls.'

'No, Max and the dogs flew out the day before yesterday to ensure our comfort while we're here. They're staying in the guest cottage down the lane.'

As the dogs romped around her, deliriously excited at the reunion, Ella could not have been more pleased by Nikolai's surprise. Although she had already been aware that Max was to continue working for them, the older man was a fabulous cook and organiser as well as being wonderfully pet friendly. His presence on the domestic front meant that Ella could totally relax.

Nikolai eyed the level in the wine glass and watched Ella reach for her water bottle. He knew the main reason why women usually stopped drinking and it sent a chill of dismay down his spine. But how could Ella possibly be pregnant? One of the qualities he most admired about Ella was her unflinching honesty and in his world that was rare indeed. Had she been pregnant he knew she would have told him immediately.

'Why have you stopped drinking?' Nikolai asked lazily.

Ella had been almost drugged by the sun-drenched scene before her. They were lying on a rug in the shade of a giant chestnut tree only a few yards from a deserted cove where unbelievably blue and clear water washed a pale sand shore. Weeks of relaxation on Crete had brought down most of Ella's defences and she only stiffened a little in receipt of that awkward question, relieved that she had an answer already prepared.

'I had a ghastly hangover a couple of months back and I just lost my taste for alcohol.'

'But why pretend to still drink?' Nikolai broke in.

Her tension soared up the scale. 'It *can* make people uncomfortable when you say you don't drink.'

'It doesn't make me uncomfortable.'

'Then I won't pretend any more,' she told him glibly but she was shocked at herself. She was actually *lying* to Nikolai and it was wrong. When had wrong begun to seem right? She had had three perfect weeks with Nikolai, without a doubt the happiest three weeks she had ever enjoyed. Even flying back to the UK to attend the funeral of the bar manager who had died in the hotel fire had not doused that happiness. Nikolai had said that she didn't need to accompany him but she had wanted to give him her support and she knew he had appreciated her presence. She had not accom-

panied him though when he had had yet another in-
terview with the police, but had shared his relief when
the police had intimated that, although they were as
yet nowhere near charging anyone for arson, they did
have leads to follow.

Back on the island Nikolai and Ella had continued
to make memories. They had visited fabled ancient Mi-
noan sites, including the archaeological dig that was
currently taking place on land Nikolai owned nearby.
They had explored Chania after dark on several eve-
nings, eating at lively *tavernas*, shopping for gifts and
visiting clubs in the old harbour area. Ella preferred the
seafront bars to the clubs once she saw how blatantly
Nikolai was besieged by predatory women drawn by
his looks and wealth. Returning from the cloakroom
to find him surrounded had been unnerving and had
ramped up her insecurity.

How attractive would Nikolai still find her once
pregnancy changed her body? There were already little
changes that only she was aware of. Her breasts were a
little bit fuller and her nipples more tender. When they
had visited the almost tropical lagoon at Elafonisi it
had become very hot and she had felt dizzy for the first
time. In a Byzantine monastery in the mountains that
glowed with colourful frescos and icons, she had felt
nauseous because they hadn't eaten in hours and Nikolai had fussed all the way down the hill to the village
café, where they had stuffed themselves full of pizza.

She had already decided to tell him about the baby
once they had returned to London. She had an almost
superstitious fear of breaking the news on their idyl-
lic honeymoon. He didn't love her. She was very, very
conscious of that, because she had been the idiot who

had involuntarily shouted out her feelings in bed one night and he had not reciprocated, although he had held her close afterwards while probably fighting the desire to apologise for not being able to return the sentiment.

And that was what she didn't want: a male who felt guilty because he *didn't* love her, because eventually that guilt would eat away at what he did feel. Even so, a man in love with his wife would be much more accepting of an unplanned pregnancy than one who merely suffered from insatiable desire. And Nikolai was insatiable with her, she conceded, a secretive smile tilting her lips as long fingers swept below the hem of her dress to stroke her thigh in a way that sent tiny hot tremors of helpless anticipation rippling through her. That seemingly unquenchable hunger of his made her feel safe. She was willing to admit that it wasn't the fairy-tale relationship she had once dreamt of having, but it was still a lot more real and passionate than anything she had ever known.

Nikolai kissed her, slow and deep, and then lifted his tousled dark head again. 'My sister, Sofia…' he framed with startling abruptness, 'committed suicide. She took an overdose. That's why I find it hard to talk about.'

Emerging from a male as reserved as Nikolai, that speech was a breakthrough and Ella gazed up at him with warmly concerned eyes. 'That must've been very tough for you to accept.'

'I didn't even know she was depressed. I hadn't seen her in months,' he explained in a bitten-off, tight undertone. 'I kept on offering to fly her over to London and she made excuses. I should've realised something was wrong and flown to her in Athens, but that was in the days before my private jet and I was working

night and day on getting my first hotel opened up. I
neglected her. I put profit first.'

'You didn't know there was anything wrong. When
you're busy time goes by and you don't notice.'

'Don't try to comfort me,' Nikolai interposed darkly.
'I let Sofia down when she needed me, the *only* time
she ever needed me. I had all these ideas about what
we would do together once I made some money, but I
should've been concentrating on the present, not the
future.'

Ella's eyes stung, for she could feel the guilty grief
he had never managed to overcome. 'You didn't know,
Nikolai, and obviously she didn't want you to know or
she'd have told you how she was feeling.'

His lean, strong face froze. 'I found out by reading
her diary. I felt bad about doing that but I needed so
badly to know…*why*…' he completed jaggedly.

'Of course you did. That's human nature,' she murmured softly, touched that he had finally chosen to
confide in her, her heart full to overflowing with love.

She still didn't know what it was about him that had
made her fall so deeply in love at such speed, she only
knew that the thought of life without him terrified her.

And in their differing ways that evening as they at-
tended a party at Nikolai's great-aunts' house in Chania, both of them mulled over that conversation and
reached certain conclusions.

After being widowed in their sixties, the twin sisters
had set up home together again and as each of them
had had several children, all of whom lived locally,
they were rarely without visitors. From their very first
visit, Nikolai and Ella had been made wonderfully welcome, long-lost members of the family being brought

back into the fold. Ella had watched Nikolai slowly unfreeze and lose the cool distrustful front that he so often wore to the world. That particular evening, Ella saw him tripping up over one of the toddlers and pausing to pick him up and dry his tears.

'He'll make a good father, unlike his own,' Dorkas Drakos pronounced with satisfaction.

'Our brother was a misery all his life. His money never brought him happiness,' Dido piped up at her sister's elbow. 'Nikolai is very different.'

Guilt was nagging at Ella as she watched Nikolai with the little boy. Maybe she shouldn't wait until they returned to London to make her announcement…

Straightening, Nikolai met his bride's luminous green eyes. He *had* to tell her the truth. She had said she loved him but had she meant it? Nikolai had never seen himself as remotely loveable. When other women had told him they loved him he had known in his bones that the only thing they really loved was his wealth and generosity, but he knew that wasn't true of Ella, who thought he spent money far too freely on her and got embarrassed whenever he gave her anything.

But to tell her the truth would entail hurting her and he had never dreaded anything more than he dreaded that prospect. If she was too badly hurt would she fall out of love again? Would she walk away? Would she never again see him in the same light? Would he irrevocably damage all that was special between them?

The more those anxieties infiltrated Nikolai, the more determined he became to clear his conscience. He didn't want to keep secrets from Ella. How could he expect her to trust him when he had yet to trust her with the truth about himself? Nor would he ever forget Ella insisting that with her he could be his *real* self. Even so that was still a major challenge for a male who had never before shown a woman his real self…

Early the following morning, however, everything changed without warning. They were having breakfast when Nikolai dug his phone out to answer a call. Ella watched his lean, darkly handsome face freeze and then saw the colour steadily draining from below his bronzed skin. His eyes cloaked as he put the phone down.

'Cyrus Makris has been arrested and charged for paying two men to set my hotel on fire and for Desmond's death,' Nikolai relayed flatly.

With the air of a sleepwalker, Nikolai rose upright and walked back indoors.

Cyrus had organised that dreadful fire? Ella was appalled and disbelieving but she did not understand Nikolai's reaction and she raced after him. 'Nikolai… what Cyrus did was unspeakable but at least the police have nailed him for it!'

Nikolai spun back to her, his dark eyes tortured. 'You don't understand. How could you? This is *my* fault… Desmond's death is down to me, no one else.'

CHAPTER TEN

As NIKOLAI STRODE off to take refuge in the room he used as an office Ella froze in place in the hall, with the dogs wandering restively round her feet. How could the fire or the bar manager's tragic death be laid at Nikolai's door? How could he possibly be thinking that way?

Nikolai turned from the window as Ella appeared in the doorway to study him with frowning bemusement. He knew he wasn't making sense. He knew she didn't get it and a great sense of weight bowed down his wide shoulders.

'Cyrus and I have been bitter enemies for a very long time,' he told her flatly.

Belatedly Ella was recalling Cyrus's sister's comment at their wedding. She had intended to ask Nikolai for further clarification but had not got around to it because at the time it hadn't seemed that important. 'Why?' she asked simply.

Nikolai's spectacular bone structure went rigid. 'He raped my sister...'

Ella paled and moved forward.

Nikolai leant back against his desk and raked long, taut fingers through his black hair, expelling his breath in a hiss. 'It was all in the diary. That's what I found out five years ago.'

Ella was filled with horror, recalling Cyrus's violent assault on her. 'What a nightmare that must have been for you.'

'Cyrus has been accused of rape before but the accusations tend to be kicked out or withdrawn or they miraculously disappear,' Nikolai advanced in a harsh undertone. 'His father is an enormously powerful and wealthy man. I looked into the cases of Cyrus's previous accusers. One of them dropped the case and now has a seat at the directors' table. She rose up the ranks at meteoric speed and is now an affluent woman who flatly refuses to discuss the matter.'

'You think she was paid off,' Ella gathered.

'Police and members of the legal profession have been bribed. A couple of other victims went from poverty to prosperity. I would assume they were compensated. But Sofia *died*,' Nikolai emphasised with pained ferocity. 'She was poor and powerless and she couldn't bear to tell me what that bastard had done to her.'

'Tell me what happened,' Ella urged quietly.

She poured Nikolai a fresh coffee on the veranda. Her hand wasn't quite steady. She was in shock about what he was telling her about Cyrus. She was remembering the way Cyrus had attacked her and suddenly taking that assault a great deal more seriously. If Nikolai was to be believed it hadn't been a momentary loss of control, the case of a man losing his temper and barely knowing what he was doing.

Sofia, Ella learned, had not enjoyed Nikolai's educational advantages and had worked in a variety of dead-end jobs before equipping herself with secretarial skills at night class. She had then taken a position as a typist in Cyrus's Athens office and one day when she was on reception he had noticed her.

Ella scanned the photo that Nikolai removed from his wallet. His sister had been truly beautiful.

'Cyrus goes for virgins. My sister was older than his usual victims but she was innocent,' Nikolai gritted, perspiration beading his upper lip as he went on to tell her how Cyrus had invited his sister out for coffee a couple of times and once to lunch, while telling her to keep their meetings secret from the people she worked with.

'I suppose that's when she should've got suspicious.' Ella sighed.

'She was naïve; thrilled and flattered that a handsome, successful man was showing an interest in her, and when he asked her to come to his apartment one evening to do some private work for him she went,' Nikolai completed.

'And that's when...right.' Ella nodded in shaken acknowledgement. 'Did Sofia go to the police afterwards?'

'Only after she had showered but the medical did show that she had been badly bruised. She was told that there wasn't enough evidence. Cyrus insisted that they had had consensual sex and he was believed and she was more or less told that she was a lonely fantasist. She felt humiliated that the police didn't believe in or support her. That's what drove her to take her own life.'

'It must have been terrifying for her,' Ella acknowledged heavily. 'I can't begin to imagine what she must have gone through.'

Nikolai was very still. 'I've spent the past five years plotting my revenge against Cyrus.'

Her smooth brow furrowing, Ella gave him a bemused look. 'Revenge?'

'After what my sister suffered, I couldn't live with the idea of Cyrus walking around unpunished. I had him investigated and, the more I learned about him, the more disgusted I became that a sexual deviant like him has never been brought to justice,' Nikolai revealed. 'To be honest, I became *obsessed* with my desire to take revenge on Cyrus…'

Ella strove to look understanding because she really couldn't blame him for his feelings after hearing the tragic story of his sister's death. Even so, the concept of revenge was so foreign to her own nature that she really couldn't grasp it at all.

'And somewhere during that five years I forgot who I was supposed to be and the man my sister had tried to raise me to be,' Nikolai admitted gravely. 'I stole business deals off Cyrus—not very satisfying. However, that was really the only damage I was able to do until his sister, Marika, phoned me a couple of months ago and informed me that Cyrus was planning to marry *you*.'

'The sister he doesn't even speak to was aware that Cyrus wanted to marry me when even I didn't suspect it?' Ella gasped, more than a little disturbed by the bombshell of her own name and connection to Cyrus Makris entering Nikolai's explanations. 'How is that possible? And why would Marika go out of her way to contact you and tell you that about me?'

'Cyrus told his father that he was planning to marry his nephew Paul's former fiancée. His father had been pressuring him to marry for some time and, after Cyrus named you, his father confided in Marika and asked her if she had ever met you. Marika contacted me because she knew that I was her brother's biggest enemy and she hates him for reasons she has never shared with me.'

Ella shook her head dully. She was getting lost in the story while sixth sense was warning her that there was something very important for her to learn from what Nikolai was telling her. Unfortunately her brain was refusing to join up the dots and pick up the clues she needed.

'When I saw your photo I couldn't believe you were the same girl I met in that car park last year,' Nikolai told her tautly.

'*When* did you see my photo?' Ella pressed, frowning as she moved restively against the wooden support post she had braced a hand on, her simple turquoise sundress swirling round her slim legs.

'As soon as I had your name I had you checked out.'

Again Ella shook her head. 'But why would you *do* that? What could Cyrus's crazy belief that he could get me to marry him possibly have to do with you?'

'I wanted to *hurt* him, Ella!' Nikolai bit out in frustration. 'I wanted to ensure that his plans for you came to nothing and that meant I had to get to you first and make you mine instead! I knew that my taking you from him would hit him hardest.'

Ella could feel the blood below her skin draining away as she finally grasped the connection he was making. Wheels within wheels and secret plotting going on behind the scenes. She could never, ever have dreamt that she owed Nikolai's keen pursuit to such a cold, merciless motivation. Indeed his pursuit had been nothing to do with her at all, nothing personal, she thought sickly, nothing personal when she so badly needed it *all* to have been personal for him.

Nikolai could hear his own heart thumping out his tension in his ears as he watched her like a hawk. She looked sick, shocked. 'I had to tell you. You have the right to know the worst about me. You need to know what and who I am and what I'm capable of.'

'Not sure I *want* to know,' Ella forced out between teeth that suddenly wanted to chatter. Her brain was in a fog. She couldn't think. She was scared to think that the male she loved could have seen her merely as a means of revenge and a weapon with which to taunt Cyrus. Was that what Nikolai was saying? Or was she picking him up wrong? Oh, dear heaven, why couldn't she think and put it all together properly?

'You married me…' she whispered shakily. '*Why* did you marry me?'

'I wanted to make you happy. After what I'd done… the blackmail, the way I treated you…the very fact that rage pushed Cyrus into attacking you. I'm the one to blame for that… I owed you.'

Of all the sentiments a woman madly in love didn't want to hear, Ella thought numbly, those three little words had to be at the top of the least popular list. *I owed you!* What was she? A debt he had to pay off? A helpless child he had to comfort and compensate? Or was the light in which he saw her even worse?

Had he guessed even before she married him how she felt about him? Had he worked out that his weapon of choice was so stupid that she had fallen in love with the blackmailing, ruthless, seven-letter-word of a man who had used her to strike a blow against his enemy?

Ella cleared her dry throat with difficulty. 'So, you had second thoughts about what you had done.'

'I felt bloody guilty!' Nikolai fired back at her in a forceful rush. 'Of course, I did. It may have taken me a while but I did eventually come to my senses and appreciate that what I had done to you was absolutely wrong on every level.'

Ella was unimpressed by those strong words.

'And is that why you made the biggest sacrifice you could think of and *married* me?' she prompted, her distress threatening to break through the false composure of shock. 'Because you were way too smart for your own good! Presumably you never planned for this marriage to last either. Well, you shot yourself in the foot bedding a virgin, Nikolai!'

'What are you talking about?' It was Nikolai's turn to look bewildered.

'A virgin has to be more likely to make a mistake concerning the efficiency of her birth control,' Ella contended, her chin tilted at an aggressive angle because she definitely didn't want to him to get the impression that she was ashamed or embarrassed or even slightly apologetic. 'I made a mistake and I'm pregnant…so sorry that doesn't fit in with your cruel, nasty, callous plans!'

His luxuriant black lashes dipped and then slowly rose again, revealing the sudden glitter in his dark eyes. 'Pregnant?' Nikolai breathed in a driven undertone, a sudden inner tide of relief making him feel almost dizzy.

If she was pregnant, he had a whole new line of reasons to argue why she should stay with him. Pregnant, he thought again, only dimly recognising the level of his own astonishment. A baby. *His* baby. After all the hints his great-aunts had dropped and he had studiously ignored, Dido and Dorkas would be ecstatic at that information.

'And the good news *is*,' Ella suddenly spat at him without warning, while his brain was still wandering all over the place in a most unfamiliar way, 'you don't *owe* me anything! The way I see it, you married me under false pretences, so we're *not* married!'

Ella wrenched at the rings on her wedding finger and flung them at his feet with bitter satisfaction. Turning on her heel, she sped off. She could feel herself coming apart like wet shredded paper inside herself and she had no intention of coming apart in front of him. She wasn't a victim; she *refused* to be a victim; she was strong. There was nothing Nikolai Drakos could throw at her that she couldn't handle, she told herself staunchly as she walked fast down the hill towards the beach.

Nikolai crouched down and lifted up her wedding and engagement rings. He was taken aback to register that his hand was shaking. He dug the rings into the pocket of his tight faded jeans. *His* baby. His baby needed her the same way he needed her. But would she be better off without him? That was a deeply wounding thought for him and he shook it off. He could be what she wanted him to be; he could deliver what she wanted him to deliver for both her *and* the baby. He would fight to keep her but he just didn't know what to say to her. He genuinely didn't know how to persuade her to stay. Ironically Nikolai had much more experience at ditching women. After all, he had never wanted to keep one for ever before.

And unhappily for him, Ella had scruples and standards and he had stomped roughly over all of them. He didn't deserve a second chance. He knew that, but admitting that he didn't deserve a second chance to her would only reinforce the wrong, negative image, he reasoned painfully. The apology front didn't look very promising either because sorry could never begin to cover the damage he had done.

Ella kicked off her shoes when she reached the shore and sank her toes into the hot sand. But her soles burned and she took off in haste for the cooler sand at the water's edge. There the sea looked so temptingly cool that she walked out into it until the lapping water was right up to her knees. She was breathing as fast as a marathon runner and her heart was pounding like mad. Calm down, she urged herself, you're pregnant.

But there was a giant ball of pain ready to explode inside Ella. Nikolai had taken her dreams and torn them apart. Once again she had placed her faith and her hopes in the wrong man. What was it about her? Was she more naïve than other women? Fatally attracted to the wrong types? And yet there was not an iota of similarity between Paul and Nikolai, so how could she have known?

Well, of course she *should* have known, another, more negative voice told her. She had gone for the fairy-tale version, hadn't she? This idea that she was so irresistible to Nikolai Drakos that he would track her down after that single meeting in the car park and settle her father's debts simply to get her into his bed? *As if!* And what sort of woman fell for the kind of guy that would blackmail a woman into his bed? And how on earth *had* she fallen for him?

By the time, Ella reached that point in her attack of self-loathing she was sobbing and the tears of heart-break were coursing down her cheeks. Where had the love come from? He had been so distraught, so devas-tated by that fire, and everything warm and caring in her had loved that in him. She had suddenly seen that the cool, detached male he pretended to be existed no place except inside his own head and the façade he wore to the world.

Only, sadly, it had not occurred to her that behind his grief for the bar manager's death at his hotel lurked a male willing to break every rule of decency and wreck a perfectly innocent woman's life in an effort to destroy an admittedly very nasty man. And he had wrecked it, Ella reasoned bitterly. He had allowed her to think that she was special to him, that he cared about her even if he hadn't given her the actual words. Didn't everyone know that most men were wary of saying the fatal words that could lead to permanent commitment?

Even so, leave it to Nikolai to find a novel slant… *I want to keep you.*

I owed you. Dear heaven, the pain of hearing that sentiment would haunt her to her dying day. So, his guilty conscience had made him offer her a wedding, a ring and the luxury of his wealth. And now here she was standing out in the sea like an idiot, she thought with another sob. It was her moment of truth, she dimly recognised. Once again she wasn't going to get the fairy-tale happy ending. Had Nikolai faked absolutely everything?

Well, he hadn't faked the sex or the insatiability factor on that front but what was that worth? He had got cuddlier too. He was actually hugging now without prompting, reaching for her hand, touching her, *always* touching her just like a besotted new husband could be expected to do. Was that all a lie as well? Some sort of a convincing act? She wiped her face with trembling hands, suddenly cold in the sunlight. He didn't love her. He hadn't moved heaven and earth to find her again or to make her his and only his. He had pursued and entrapped her *only* to punish Cyrus. That was always going to be her bottom line.

Nikolai saw her standing in the sea and sheer panic controlled him. Later he didn't remember running down the hill, racing through the orange groves and taking a flying leap down onto the beach instead of following the path. He waded out into the water and snatched her up into his arms just as the sound of his splashing approach began to turn her head.

Bronze-coloured hair fell down over his arm. Slightly pink-edged green eyes gazed up at him in astonishment. 'What are you doing?'

Nikolai couldn't find his voice. He strode up the beach and sank down on the steep edge of the path with Ella still tightly cradled in his arms.

'Let me go!' she exclaimed.

'Not until I know for sure you're all right.'

Against her cheek she could feel his heart thumping very fast and he was breathing heavily. 'I don't know what you're talking about.'

'You were standing out in the sea. It scared me,' he acknowledged gruffly.

'You think I'd do something silly to myself and my

baby over what you've done?' Ella pelted back at him, going from tearful acquiescence to rage in the space of seconds as she finally understood his concern. 'Are you out of your mind? I spent years watching Paul struggle and fight to live. Life is a very precious thing!'

Nikolai breathed again but he still didn't want to let go of her. 'The baby…how long have you known?'

Ella stopped struggling to escape. 'The day before the wedding I discovered that my implant was old and inactive by the time we…had sex,' she framed with cold precision.

'It wasn't only sex. It was something rather more meaningful.'

'Says the man who wouldn't know meaningful from a slap in the face!'

'Why didn't you tell me you were pregnant?' Nikolai persisted, hitting her on her weakest flank. 'Why, in fact, did you come very close to lying in an effort to deflect my questions about why you weren't drinking alcohol?'

'No comment.' Ella buttoned her lips together.

'We can just sit here,' Nikolai conceded in a remarkably level voice.

'I'm all wet now—and you're even more wet!' she cried.

Silence fell, backed by the soft rush and retreat of the surf on the beach.

'I can't bear to lose you,' Nikolai volunteered gruffly. 'I'll do anything it takes to keep you.'

'My goodness, the sex must be stupendous,' Ella told him acidly, her attention involuntarily on his lean, dark, utterly gorgeous face while she scolded herself for even noticing.

He was beautiful but deceptive like a crisp, glossy apple with a rotten core, she told herself doggedly.

'It is,' Nikolai agreed. 'But we've got a lot more than that between us. You know we have.'

'I don't know anything about you any more.'

'I believe that if you stop and really think about it you'll realise that you know much more than you're prepared to admit right now. Obviously you know I'm not perfect.'

'Do you want a slow hand clap or a rousing cheer for that remarkably shrewd deduction?'

Glittering dark eyes assailed hers without warning. 'Do you want to be dropped back into the sea from a height?' Nikolai asked, his arms tightening suggestively round her slight body.

Ella closed her eyes tight, feeling a flush sting her tear-stung face and gritting her teeth. He had said he would do anything to keep her but he wasn't prepared to lie down and be kicked, which was all she wanted to do to him at that moment. She wasn't feeling forgiving or constructive or even like talking, she was simply feeling hurt. 'I want to go back up to the house if you won't leave me alone down here.'

Nikolai expelled his breath and slowly set her down on her own feet, almost as if he was afraid that without his support she might fall over. As he swept up the sandals she had abandoned earlier and painstakingly put them on for her an embittered laugh bubbled in Ella's throat. She held it in though, thinking she had to support herself, go forward, face the future as it was, not as she had wished and dreamt it might be. As she walked silently back to the house, she was conscious of her exhaustion and knew she needed to lie down. All that emotional turmoil had extracted a high cost in terms of her energy levels.

Nikolai followed Ella upstairs.

'Going to bed for a while,' she muttered limply, trying to slam the door in his face.

'Let me help you...'

Ella swallowed back the bitter comment that nothing he could do or say would help her state of mind. Some pain went too deep to be soothed by even the kindest gesture. He felt guilty and she knew that, recognised that, but she didn't want to have to deal with his guilt. That was *his* problem and she had enough to cope with. She pulled off her dress, letting it lie where it fell, shimmied out of her underwear and clambered into the bed naked.

'Do you want some tea?' Nikolai suggested, rearranging the duvet over her quite unnecessarily. 'I *can* make tea.'

Ella shut her eyes, fatigue dragging her down like a strong current in the sea. She wanted to sleep, she wanted to forget and she couldn't forget while he was around. 'No, thanks.'

Nikolai sank down silently on a chair in the corner of the bedroom. She was as white as a sheet and her eyes looked haunted, bruised, *hurt*. It was what he had most feared and it felt even worse than he had expected because he felt helpless and he wasn't used to being helpless. But he had had to tell her, he reminded himself heavily; she had deserved the truth rather than some fanciful fiction. It occurred to him that she hadn't yet heard the *whole* truth, but then she probably wouldn't believe him, would she?

Ella wakened to find Nikolai standing over her. 'You have to put these on.'

She surfaced from sleep and instantly remembered all that had happened but she had no idea why Nikolai was trying to induce her to put on a pair of winter pyjamas. 'Why?'

'The doctor is waiting downstairs to come up and check you over.'

'The doctor?' she gasped, sitting up and reaching for the ridiculous pyjamas in a rush. 'Why have you called a doctor?'

'Because you've had a major emotional upset and you're pregnant and you need to be careful,' Nikolai told her stubbornly. 'I'm doing what I'm supposed to do. I'm trying to look after you.'

'Yeah, push me down, walk over me, drag me up again,' Ella framed bitterly. 'That's great looking after on your part.'

'Mr Theodopoulos is the leading gynaecologist on the island. Dorkas and Dido recommended him.'

'So now they know I'm carrying a baby as well,' Ella mumbled resentfully.

'I'm proud that you are,' Nikolai declared, startling her as he plumped up the pillows behind her and twitched the duvet even higher. 'The doctor is young for his position. Perhaps you would prefer an older man or...even a woman?' he extended almost hopefully.

It was no surprise to Ella then that the gynaecologist who appeared enjoyed movie-star good looks and the kind of warm, soothing bedside manner that put a woman instantly at her ease while at the same time riling a possessive husband. Nikolai behaved like a dog with a juicy bone under threat. He insisted on staying and then paced grim-faced at the back of the room with folded arms, monitoring every smile the doctor won from his wife.

Of course, there was nothing to worry about where her health was concerned. Early pregnancy was tiring and that was all that was the matter with her.

Ella was in the shower when Nikolai came back upstairs after seeing the doctor off. She towelled herself dry in the cubicle and then stepped out, refusing to act self-conscious even though it no longer felt right to be naked around him.

'You don't look pregnant,' Nikolai observed.

'Of course I don't. I'm only a few weeks along. There won't be much sign of anything for a month or so yet. Don't you know that?' she asked, pulling clothing out of the closet while studiously ignoring him in the hope that he would recognise that his presence was inappropriate.

'No. I know absolutely nothing about pregnancy,' Nikolai admitted. 'But I can find out.'

'Don't push yourself on my account,' Ella flipped back drily.

'Why didn't you tell me sooner?' he pressed while she stood at the vanity combing through her wet hair.

'I was shocked. When we discussed us starting a family you weren't exactly enthusiastic about the concept of becoming a father,' Ella reminded him flatly. 'I assumed it would upset you and I didn't want that this early in our marriage. Of course, I didn't know that there was an even bigger elephant hiding in the room!'

Nikolai settled her rings down on the counter at her elbow. 'Please put your rings back on...'

'No,' Ella countered flatly, her lips compressed.

'After I first met you in that car park and you turned me down I ran like hell away from you,' Nikolai breathed, startling her. 'I think on some level I knew that if I got involved with you it was going to turn into something I wasn't ready for.'

'You have some imagination, Nikolai. Telling me that you ran like hell isn't exactly a compliment,' Ella pointed out.

'But it's the truth.'

'The truth is that you *only* looked me up again because Cyrus took a strange fancy to me,' Ella reminded him as she walked out of the bathroom back into the bedroom.

'I was obsessed by my need for revenge. I took no account of anything else. For five years I lived, breathed and slept revenge. I was very angry and bitter about Sofia and I think it was like poison in my brain.'

'And together we're toxic,' Ella slotted in, refusing to be persuaded.

'Max has lunch ready for us downstairs.' Nikolai pulled open the bedroom door.

The table on the veranda was beautifully set. The honeymoon couple's dream lunch served on exquisite china amid flowers and crystal. She breathed in deep, the dogs nudging a welcome against her ankles, and she paused for a moment to give them some attention.

Nikolai saw that having three or four legs, a shaggy coat and a tail bought advantages he couldn't dream of acquiring. He breathed in deep and slow, reminding himself of the positives. She hadn't gone for the suitcases yet, hadn't mentioned flying anywhere. He was terrified that she would want to leave Crete and him behind.

'We're not toxic,' he declared, pouring some water for her. 'And I wouldn't have got "upset" about the baby. Like you, I'm very practical. That's something we have in common. It is what it is and we can both adapt to suit a new situation.'

'I *loved* you!' Ella slung at him without the smallest warning.

Nikolai shrank from the past tense. 'The dynamic changed between us very fast. I had no plans beyond taking you to that charity function and moving you into the town house. Somewhere about there I lost control of everything...'

'Are you trying to excuse yourself for having sex with me?' Ella enquired in a glacial voice.

His dark deep-set eyes flashed gold. 'No. I'd be a complete liar if I said I had regrets about that. In fact you pretty much owned me from that day on.'

'*Owned* you?' Ella repeated emphatically. 'Because of the sex?'

Nikolai sank an entire glass of wine. It was *so* difficult. He had never done anything so difficult as trying to talk to Ella in the mood she was currently in. 'Hardly,' he deflected. 'I suspect that's when I fell in love with you. You snuggled up to me in bed and, although I didn't admit it to myself, I liked it. I still really like it when you do that and it's so peculiar for me to like something like that...'

Ella almost dropped the glass in her hand. She stared at him, colour rising in her cheeks. 'You're lying, of course you're lying. You're still in guilty-conscience mode and you know I love you, so you're telling me what you think I want to hear.'

'But you don't *want* to hear it,' Nikolai pointed out

helplessly. 'You only want to sit there judging me and deciding that I am a total bastard in every way. And I was a bastard before I met you.'

'*And* when you first met me *and* when you met me a second time,' Ella reminded him.

'But I changed. You changed me. Don't ask me how. It happened and here I am and I'm as obsessed with you now as I once was with Cyrus,' Nikolai completed fiercely. 'I don't do or plan anything without thinking about you. You're always inside my head.'

Ella was finally starting to listen. Even the dogs were listening because Nikolai had a piece of baguette in his hand and he was waving his hands around as he spoke and the dogs were very hopeful that that piece of bread would fall in their direction. *'Really?'*

'Yes, *really*,' Nikolai derided. 'I'm crazy about you.'

'You have a funny way of showing it.'

'I couldn't love you and not tell you the truth. That wouldn't have been fair.'

Ella studied him, slowly, almost painfully registering his sincerity, his certainty. He really believed that he loved her now. He really, truly believed that. 'When I told you that I loved you, you said nothing,' she reminded him.

'I had to tell you the truth first but I was… I was…'

'What?' she broke in impatiently.

'Scared… OK? Satisfied now?' Nikolai raked back at her angrily. 'I was scared I would lose you but I couldn't live with keeping a secret like that from you.'

Ella went pink and dropped her head. 'Oh,' she almost whispered, wondering why she was being so hard on him.

Yes, he had hurt her but she appreciated his respect

for the truth, his inability to stay quiet and pretend that everything was all right when it wasn't. She breathed in slow and deep. Nikolai Drakos loved her… Nikolai *loved* her. A tiny ping of happiness cut through her grey cloud of heartbroken misery and regret. She was scared to feel happy, scared to trust him. But Nikolai had pretty much felt the same way, she reasoned wryly. Love didn't come with guarantees any more than people did. And yes, he was far from perfect, but then she wasn't perfect either and she loved him so very much it hurt to have a table separating them. Slowly she rose to her feet.

Sensing a change in the atmosphere, Nikolai surveyed her warily. 'I can make this up to you. I do know I messed up really badly—'

'Shut up,' Ella told him, tipping herself down into his lap. 'It's done and dusted and when I told you that I loved you I meant it. I love you even when you mess things up. I may get angry and shout and throw my rings at you…but at the end of it all I will still love you very, very much. As long as the mess up doesn't involve another woman,' she qualified hastily, lest he think he could be forgiven for any sin.

Nikolai wrapped both arms round her very tightly and dropped a kiss on the top of her head. 'No other women,' he said gruffly, because he could hardly get breath into his deflated lungs. 'I need all my energy for you.'

Ella gazed up at him with a smile that was like the sun breaking through the clouds. 'So… I *own* you?'

His eyes were melted caramel. 'That's what it feels like sometimes.'

'No, that's being part of a couple,' she argued, hugging him back with all her strength, tears prickling in her eyes because she was experiencing the most enormous sense of relief. He had given her the fairy tale by falling in love with her and he didn't understand how it had happened any better than she did, but that didn't matter, did it?

'Are we hoping for a boy or a girl?' Nikolai asked, long fingers splaying across her defiantly flat stomach.

'We don't get to choose. I don't mind either way,' she muttered abstractedly as she brushed her lips back and forth very gently across his.

'Neither do I...' Nikolai growled, rising from the chair with her still gripped in his arms. 'You can have a dozen kids if I get to keep you.'

'Not thinking in terms of that many,' Ella declared, succumbing to a passionate kiss that sent tingles all the way to her toes. 'Are we going to bed?'

'Can't wait to make you mine again, *latria mou*,' Nikolai husked against her reddened lips. 'You gave me such a scare today. I need to know you're still my wife. You have to put your rings back on.'

'I'll think about it,' she teased, revelling in the sense of power he was giving her because it was wonderful to know and accept that she was so wanted, so loved, so valued.

'When I married you my only wish was to make you happy,' he admitted. 'And then *today*—'

'That's behind us now,' Ella interrupted. 'And you're about to make me incredibly happy by telling me that you love me again.'

'Do I really have to keep on saying it?' Nikolai groaned.

'Yes, that's your penance...' Ella whispered as he

laid her down on their bed and stared down at her with a fierce appreciation she could feel right down to the marrow of her bones. Yes, he loved her. She could see it, she could feel it and it felt amazing…

EPILOGUE

TOBIAS DRAKOS, FIVE years old and a bundle of lively energy who was rarely still, raced downstairs in advance of his mother. Taking note that the front door of the country house, Tayford Hall, already stood wide with Max at the ready to greet his employer, Tobias crowed. 'I told you it was the helicopter, Mummy... I told you it was Daddy!'

Ella studied her son, the very image of his father with his above-average height, dark eyes and dark hair, and suppressed a groan because she knew that she would never get him to bed early now. That would have been acceptable any other night but it was Christmas Eve and she had loads of things she wanted to do while Tobias was upstairs and out of sight. Even so, he hadn't seen his father in a full week, which was a good enough excuse to loosen up on routine.

Ella knew that if she had a fault it was her tendency to stick too close to routine. But she and Nikolai led very busy lives, and without a routine someone or something got short-changed. Rory and Butch were already racing across the lawn in pursuit of their offspring, Maxie, the only one of Rory's litter of puppies they had kept. Maxie was an indiscriminate mixture of doggy genes and she had grown into a much leggier and larger dog than her diminutive parents. Before Ella could say a word, her son had raced out across the lawn in his pyjamas just as the helicopter landed.

Ella stayed circumspectly on the top step, although to tell the truth she would have been much happier pelting across the lawn with dogs and child because Nikolai rarely travelled these days and when he did she missed him terribly. And there he was, her for-ever-and-ever guy, tall and dark and handsome, striding towards her with over-excited dogs bouncing in his path and a son talking a mile a minute to him.

As Nikolai hitched Tobias up and hugged him, her heart constricted because she loved to see them together like that. Nikolai had had so many insecurities about becoming a parent but, like many goal-driven men, he had exceeded her expectations in that role. He tried to ensure that his son received everything he himself had been denied by neglectful parents. He gave Tobias his time, showed an interest and supported the little boy at every step of his development.

Ella smoothed down her scarlet knee-length dress and shifted in her very high-heeled shoe-boots, slender legs braced as Nikolai drew closer and his lean, darkly handsome features came into focus. Her whole body lit up like a firework display because just seeing Nikolai made her that happy and she had news to share that made her even happier.

Nikolai studied the picture Ella made at the front door and thought that he was an incredibly lucky man. Behind her the welcome of the house and the edge of the sparkling Christmas tree in the hall with its roaring log fire made him smile. He had bought the hall when Ella was pregnant and she adored country life. Once she had qualified as a veterinary surgeon, she had taken a job nearby and had become very popular in the local community. If he didn't watch over her she worked too hard, and now that she had her career and Tobias had started school if he went away on business he had to travel alone, which he disliked.

Nikolai swept Ella theatrically into his arms, melted-caramel eyes brimming with amusement. 'What have you done with my wife?' he teased. 'The last time I saw you, your hair was a mess, you were wearing a lab coat and wellies and now you look like a model.'

'And it took hours so appreciate it while you can,' Ella advised him while quietly revelling in the familiar scent of him and the feel of his lean, powerful body even briefly in contact with her own. A familiar burn sparked deep inside her, a burn and an ache that would have to go unsatisfied until much later in the evening because they had a houseful of guests to look after. Gramma and her father were staying for Christmas, as were Dido and Dorkas, Nikolai's great-aunts, and an array of other Greek family members, whom Nikolai and Ella had grown particularly friendly with during their frequent stays in the house on Crete.

'I find you sexy in anything. Naked, clothed, it doesn't matter, *latria mou*,' her husband assured her under cover of their son's chatter, lean fingers spreading caressingly on her hip. 'I'm shockingly lacking in standards in that line. I'll take you any way I can have you.'

Ella risked a quick kiss that smudged her lipstick and turned into something a little longer than either of them planned.

'That's not cool, Dad,' Tobias pronounced in disgust.

A highly amused grin slashed Nikolai's expressive mouth. 'I can assure you that it was very cool. We can catch up while I get changed,' he told his wife, grabbing her hand and only pausing on the stairs to greet his father-in-law and Gramma.

'I should be downstairs being a hostess,' Ella hissed guiltily.

'When you put Gramma with my great-aunts, we're coming down with hostesses who love to host. Anyway, I have something to tell you,' he announced, thrusting open their bedroom door. 'About Cyrus.'

'Cyrus?' Ella repeated in surprise, because she rarely thought now about the older man, who had received a lengthy prison sentence for his role in the hotel fire and the death of Nikolai's bar manager. While on bail for those crimes, Cyrus had also been accused of rape by a young woman in his employ and he had been found guilty of that offence as well.

'He's apparently in hospital after an attack by fellow inmates. He's not expected to survive,' Nikolai informed her flatly. 'Marika phoned me to tell me.'

'And how does that make you feel?' Ella prompted anxiously.

'As though it really is all over now and I can put it behind me,' Nikolai confessed. 'When his sentence was extended because of the rape, I felt that my sister was finally vindicated and I haven't really thought about Makris since then.'

'That's how it should be. *It's over.*' Ella wrapped her arms round him and rested her head against his chest, loving the reassuring beat of his heart and the heat of him on a cold wintry evening. 'We have more positive matters on our agenda.'

'Oh… I get it. You thought I only brought you up here to throw you on the bed? How could you think that?' Nikolai demanded, struggling to look offended.

'Because I know your sleek, sneaky ways, Mr Drakos,' Ella told him lovingly. 'No, I have other news. I'm pregnant again and this time around I'm telling you the same day I found out.'

Nikolai swung her up into his arms and kissed her with passionate satisfaction. They had waited to extend their family until their lives were more settled, but conception had taken several months longer than they had initially hoped. 'That's the best Christmas present yet!' he swore.

'No, that was our first Christmas when you brought me here to this house and told me it was ours,' Ella contradicted.

'And you were enraged that I'd picked a house and the furniture without getting you involved,' Nikolai reminded her.

'You did remarkably well on your own,' Ella said as she freed him of his tie and began to push his jacket off his shoulders. 'Take your clothes off, Mr Drakos.'

'I love it when you get domineering,' Nikolai teased, gazing down at his tiny wife with hotly appreciative dark eyes. 'I love you, *latria mou.*'

'I love you too…'

And they kissed, initially tenderly and then more

passionately. The three elderly ladies downstairs were terrific hostesses and ensured that dinner was put back until the owners of the house had reappeared with a noticeable glow of happy contentment surrounding them.

* * * * *

If you enjoyed
LYNNE GRAHAM'S 100TH STORY,
check out this author's other great reads

THE SICILIAN'S STOLEN SON
LEONETTI'S HOUSEKEEPER BRIDE
THE GREEK COMMANDS HIS MISTRESS
THE GREEK DEMANDS HIS HEIR
THE SHEIKH'S SECRET BABIES
Available now!

#3445 BOUGHT BY HER ITALIAN BOSS
by Dani Collins
Vittorio Donatelli will do anything to protect his company from scandal—he's kept the secret of his true parentage hidden for years. So if it means making stunning Gwyn his mistress to combat the vicious rumors, then he'll do it...with pleasure.

#3446 THE UNWANTED CONTI BRIDE
The Legendary Conti Brothers
by Tara Pammi
If Sophia Rossi wants to save her father's business, then merging the Rossi and Conti empires is the only way. Except Luca Conti broke Sophia's heart once before and can still make her body tremble with just a look!

#3447 MASTER OF HER INNOCENCE
Bought by the Brazilian
by Chantelle Shaw
After it's revealed that Clare Marchant is only disguised as a nun to save her kidnapped sister, Diego suddenly finds himself trading his prize diamond to help her. Now Clare is indebted to the notorious womanizer and he intends to collect...

#3448 THE FLAW IN RAFFAELE'S REVENGE
by Annie West
Relentless Italian Raffaele Petri needs reclusive researcher Lily Nolan to see his revenge plans come to fruition. But the damaged beauty is feisty, argumentative and all too intriguing to be ignored!

YOU CAN FIND MORE INFORMATION ON UPCOMING HARLEQUIN® TITLES, FREE EXCERPTS AND MORE AT WWW.HARLEQUIN.COM.

HPCNM0616RB

The car pulled up at her hotel and Abby wondered if he'd
suggest dinner and if she might accept.

But Matteo, being Matteo, skipped the entrée, main
and dessert and, after such a lovely day, for him the
ending was inevitable.

"We could," Matteo said, "always go to mine."

That delicious mouth moved in for the kill and what
startled Abby the most was that she wanted to accept, to
just close her eyes and give in to the bliss he offered,
except she jerked her head back.

"I'm assuming we're not talking about the restaurant
at your hotel?"

"We're not."

For Matteo, sex was as straightforward and as simple
as that.

"What happened to keeping it strictly business?" Abby
asked.

"I can juggle both."

He looked into green eyes that had been relaxed and smiling all day but now had turned to sleet.

"I'll see you on race day." Abby's voice was tart. He could feel the anger and indignation emanating from her, and Matteo, who only ever played with the willing, leaned back. "If you're still interested, that is." She didn't wait for the driver to open the door for her; instead she got out and slammed it shut.

You're not here to seduce, Matteo reminded himself as the driver took his rarely rejected passenger back to his hotel.

Matteo never misread signs.

Today the two of them had blasted a heat to rival a Dubai sun.

It was better this way, he conceded as he climbed out of the car and headed to his luxury suite.

If ever he'd been glad that he hadn't told Abby about the necklace, it was now, because he was seriously interested in the Boucher racing team.

And, far more worryingly for Matteo, he was also seriously interested in Abby herself.

Which was, for a die-hard bachelor, very troubling indeed.

Don't miss
DI SIONE'S INNOCENT CONQUEST
by Carol Marinelli,
available July 2016 wherever
Harlequin Presents® books and ebooks are sold.

www.Harlequin.com